Crashing into Love

Harmony Noble

TrueLoveWriters

Revised Edition: March 2024

ISBN 979-8-9884714-8-6, 978-1-963074-60-4 & ISBN 979-8-9884714-6-2

Story creation, cover, and illustrations by Melody Noble & Harmony Curtis

Thank you for choosing this book.
We hope the story
brought you as much joy reading it
as we had in creating it!

We'd love to hear from you! Feel free to reach out via email at TrueLoveWriters@gmail.com, and follow us on Instagram, Facebook, TikTok at @truelovewriters for the latest updates and behind-the-scenes fun.

Get access to exclusive offers, bonus content, new release updates, and recommendations for more great reads.

Sign up for our e-newsletter at HarmonyNoble.com.

To **YOU**, my Cherished Reader,

This journey wouldn't be as heartwarming and vibrant without you by my side. Your unwavering support, laughter, and sharing my success breathed life into these pages, transforming mere words into a tapestry of an experience. Your dedication to my stories pushes me to craft tales that resonate deeply and evoke emotions making this rom-com unforgettable. As you dive into the world I've created, I invite you to enjoy traveling to Alaska, the excitement of new love, and the joy of every heartfelt connection.

Whether you're sipping a latte by the fire, embracing the outdoors, or simply enjoying a quiet moment, know that this novel dedication is for you—the dreamers, the romantics, the seekers of joy.

THANK YOU for being a part of this incredible journey, and for allowing me to share my passion with you.

I look forward to bringing you more sweet, compelling romances.

Crashing into Love

Harmony Noble

TrueLoveWriters

Chapter 1

Nurse Riley

Holy Moose Balls!

The frozen earth advances towards me, a terrifying, surreal situation stealing the air from my lungs. The tiny two-seater plane fills with a strangling invisible weight while a spine-chilling paralysis pins my body to the seat.

Shaking, I shut my eyes, clinging to the hope that this is a dream. Dying on my first day working as an Alaskan village nurse wasn't in the job description.

"Wake Up, Riley," I silently say to myself.

A violent jolt causes my eyes to snap open, jerking me back to reality. With my stomach in my throat and my heart racing, the ground rushes towards me.

This is no dream!

Desperation propels me to whirl around, facing Trevor, the young Alaskan pilot. I need reassurance, a comforting smile, or a nod to signal that I'm overreacting-this is normal for an Alaskan bush flight. After all, flying in a tiny two-seater bush plane is a new experience.

"Mayday. *Mayday!* We're going down. Our heading is Southwest into the mountains. Does anyone read me? MAYDAY!" Trevor's frantic voice blasts through my headset, amplifying my panic.

My silent plea is unheard, and drawing in a gasping breath, I tell myself, *I will not die today.*

The roaring propeller reverberates, shaking me to my core. Despite wearing the bulky noise-canceling headset, doom's muted sounds overwhelm me. The plane's sporadic jerks, Trevor's amplified voice, and my body slammed against the cold window, watching the jagged peaks reaching for us juxtaposes the sight, minutes ago, of the picturesque salmon spawning stream winding through the mountain.

I should close my eyes and pray but lock eyes with Trevor instead. His wild gaze meets mine, and I project confidence, hoping he'll absorb some to find a way out of this nosedive. My nursing school wisdom echoes in my mind — no matter the emergency, fake confidence and stay calm, and everything will work out.

We will survive.

His panicked eyes look away as he grapples with the steering column, desperately scanning the controls.

"He's getting the plane under control, and we're landing safely in Portlock," I whisper to myself like a prayer.

Moments before, Trevor made a grand detour to impress me with his aerial acrobatics between the mountains. Between his boasts of future private jet escapades and racing sports cars, his egocentric banter escalated my concerns about his unprofessionalism. Not to mention, he looks more like a frat boy than a capable pilot.

At boarding, I dismissed my initial unease as nervous excitement for starting my new career. Trevor casually checked off the pre-flight list without consulting his instruments or gauges. My gut knotted, telling me it was a mistake. I should have trusted my instincts—I saw the red flags but chose to stay. Now, I'm stuck beside him, going down off-course in the remote wilderness with no souls in sight.

His relentless flirting and invasive touching during the flight intensified my discomfort. If I had batted my eyelashes and giggled at his asinine jokes, I'd be safe in Portlock instead of zigzagging around the mountainside. Our plane should have landed by now.

Instead, I remained professional, firmly redirecting him and ignoring his flirting. "Can you please take me directly to Portlock?" I had requested for the second time, hoping to be on time for my community flu clinic, which only caused him to double down on showing off with his hot dogging. Trevor's relentless pursuit of a date and my response backfired.

But appeasing men isn't my forte. I chose this remote nursing position to immerse myself in my medical career, avoiding dating distractions. The relentless pursuit by guys like Trevor, who only see me as a hot blonde, validates my decision.

Our exchanges have spiraled us off course, far from Portlock, and my frustration grows. This is not the thrilling Alaskan nursing adventure I envisioned for my first day. If only I had given in to his advances, we would have landed in Portlock by now. This is not the thrilling Alaskan nursing adventure I imagined for my first day!

In reality, I didn't choose a village job to avoid all men. In actuality, my desire to help fellow Alaskans is the driving force behind becoming a nurse. My mom is a nurse, and in nursing school, I learned that remote villages desperately needed nurses. And I want to make a difference which village nursing provides.

Staring at the looming mountain, I take a shuddering breath, my thoughts on my mom—she warned me against accepting this village job and wanted me to work in the plush surgical center with her.

"Plane 2467. Sir, pull up. You're too low for the approach. Plane 2467, Pull. Up," the calm air traffic controller's voice, laced with a Yup'ik Alaskan silkiness, streams through our headsets. Her steady tone, gentle and commanding, cuts through the chaotic sounds, bringing a sense of confidence and calm to our deadly descent.

As the potential disaster looms, her unshakable confidence resonates through her powerful cadence, steering us away from a fiery crash in the remote Alaskan wilderness.

I shift my gaze from the mountain's rocky face to the stream, pondering which crash landing is worse. But I shake off the morbid thoughts.

Snap out of it, Riley! Focus on her voice. You are not dying. Especially not next to this showoff jerk.

Without a doubt, my calling is to be a village nurse, just as I know her confident voice directing us through my headset will lead us to safety. Furthermore, when we touch down, I'm hugging the woman behind the voice who will save me.

With determination, I seize the steering yoke alongside Trevor, planting my feet on the control panel and willing the plane upward. The aircraft shudders, responding to our efforts, and gradually levels. A final tremor releases us from the mountain's jagged grip. Trevor maneuvers skillfully, steering away from treetops and banking us over the rushing stream.

"ShitFuckerEatingHell..." he mutters through my headset, and I can't help but roll my eyes at his colorful language in the face of impending disaster.

Suddenly, the plane glides smoothly under Trevor's control, a metal bird soaring above the pristine mountainside. He lets out a whoop. "Now that, Sugarpie, is how you fly!" He grabs my leg, squeezes, and playfully nudges my hands off the yoke.

I slump back into my seat, drained, sucking in air to calm my thundering pulse, still trembling, and with fiery lungs slowly releasing to allow oxygen in. *I'm going to make it.*

"2467. What is your status? 2467. Report. Over," the air traffic controller's calm voice asks through the headset.

"We're sightseeing over the river and heading in. I'll be landing on airstrip one eastward. Roger that, over," Trevor responds confidently, shooting me a wink as if our near-death experience was just another Tuesday.

"Negative, 2467. Gain altitude and circle to land *westward* on airstrip one, over. Airstrip one. Over," she instructs, her voice guiding us into Portlock.

"Fine, Mary. Airstrip One," Trevor replies casually with a frown, sliding his hand through his hair.

My heart is settling, but my hands are still clenched in fists despite the now-controlled flight into Portlock.

"Hey, most people pay a fortune for an airshow. You're quite a lucky girl. Did you see the brown bear in the creek? Ballin'!" he grins, pushing his dark, mirrored aviator glasses up to cover his eyes.

"You..." I start but stop before finishing with *Asshole! You almost killed me. Land the darn plane already.*

I bite my tongue, refraining from distracting or provoking him and risking another round of mountain circling. His type thrives on challenges—I won't feed his fragile ego. I'll keep quiet, and I'm not flirting back.

When I discussed the job with Nurse Kathy, the Alaskan Community Health Program Director, she warned me about the challenges of Alaskan village nursing. She also emphasized the hazards of dealing with bush pilots. Kathy, a no-nonsense woman, didn't mince words about how these young pilots caused headaches with their arrogance and disregard for culture.

"These bush pilots are city boys, amassing flight hours to land bigger, lucrative airliner gigs," she explained, her frustration evident in her voice.

"They're horny and self-absorbed, completely clueless about village culture. Dealing with their attitudes causes unnecessary headaches for *everyone*. Just ignore and tolerate them, like the villagers do. They depend on these flights for their mail, and supplies, or they wouldn't tolerate the outsiders' attitude. We need them to get into the villages since there aren't any roads or boats to get to most of our villages."

As my heart settles into a regular rhythm, I glance at Trevor, smirking. I tried to ignore him and remain professional, but Kathy's warning was right. And dangerous or not, Trevor is my only ride into Portlock today. I must endure his egotism for the flight, but I'm not encouraging his arrogant antics—*absolutely not.*

Being raised by a single-working mom, I know I don't need a partner. If I *choose* to date, it'll be with someone affectionate and supportive. As a nurse, I need a safe, nurturing partner, and Trevor is the opposite of that, a hotshot narcissist. *No way would I ever date him.*

The brush with death has my head spinning, but my resolve stands strong - I don't need a partner. I'm focused on my nursing career, aiming to climb the ranks and become the Alaska Community Health Director in the next decade. Dating or flirting is off the table—I'm too busy for distractions, and a plane crash is definitely not in my schedule.

"Here's my car." Trevor pulls out his expensive phone, showing me a tripped-out red Camaro with him posing behind the wheel.

He switches tactics, unable to impress me with his piloting. I continue ignoring him and focus on getting off this plane alive. *No, thank you, Asshole. I'm not playing your game.* "Um, sorry. My hands are full," I say, refusing the phone he's pressing into my hand. I bet next, he'll try showing me his flexing photos *or worse.*

I gather my scattered Portlock medical binder pages from the floor, organizing them meticulously. Portlock is small enough that every patient's data sheet fits in the binder, along with my nursing protocols and paperwork for managing today's flu vaccination clinic.

Trevor, seemingly undeterred, shrugs, places his phone back, and radios the air traffic controller. "2467 approaching for landing on airstrip one, over."

"Copy, 2467," Mary responds, her soothing voice a balm to my nerves.

Moments later, he guides the plane onto the desolate gravel strip without further drama.

My subtle hints got through to him as he refrained from flashing me more pictures or attempting to flirt.

Stopped on the dark, barren strip, I anticipate his next move and quickly unbuckle myself before he can fumble with my chest strap.

He flips open the plane's exit, a surprisingly large side window. With a swift move, he clambers onto the wing and jumps to land on the icy gravel runway.

I grab my shoulder bag, and despite my initial inclination to ignore his proffered hand, I reluctantly accept it, allowing him to assist me in stepping from the plane's wing to the solid ground.

At last, I've escaped the confines of this metal coffin and the insufferable presence of its pilot.

My legs wobble, and a lightheaded sensation envelops me, even with my feet firmly planted on the ground.

I thank the stars. I've survived the nerve-wracking flight, and I'm safely in Portlock.

Chapter 2

Nurse Riley

After the cocky pilot helps me clamber from the small plane, he takes hold of my hands. Trevor gazes at me, his blue eyes brimming with anticipation, and his mouth quirks up at the corners.

What's he waiting for? A tip? My digits?

He's delusional if he thinks he's getting anything from me. He's lucky I'm a polite professional, or I'd punch him in his smug mouth for his abhorrent behavior.

"My bags?" I ask with a tight smile, which doesn't reach my eyes as I shake my hands loose.

Trevor frowns, pockets his phone, and lifts his chin, insulted. He's dealing with the unexpected, a woman not gushing thank you's and promising a handsome pilot her virginity for the flight into the tiny Alaskan village.

Reminding myself of the geographical reality—Portlock is landlocked in the Alaskan bush, inaccessible by roads or ferries—I add through gritted teeth, "Trevor, it's a pleasure to meet you. Thank you for the flight." Remaining professional is paramount, even with someone as insufferable as him.

"Yeah, sure, whatever. I gotta nab the mail totes," he grumbles, turning away.

I nod, casting my eyes over the gravel airstrip. The lone metal-arched building about twenty yards away must be the airport facility, and the approaching truck likely belongs to the Village Elder coming to welcome me.

"Gimme your number. I'll take you out when we're back to civilization. I'm on the VIP list of some very exclusive clubs in Anchorage," he suggests, creeping beside me, an annoyance like a stray hair floating in my Starbucks mocha.

Seriously?! His relentless flirtations are bordering on harassment.

Does he hound women until they surrender, worn down by his relentless advances?

Before I can respond, the grumbling old Bronco truck rumbles up to greet us.

"Trevor, you Asshole!"

I instantly relax as I recognize the previously gentle voice and instantly forget my annoyance with him. The woman who calmed me and guided us to safety is here, and the mere encounter makes my heart pound. Her melodic voice envelops me in warmth, countering the chilly air.

Who is this Yup'ik woman scolding Trevor?

"Mary!" Trevor calls out, attempting to fist-bump her. Mary towers over him, stoically refusing to raise her hand, leaving his fist hanging awkwardly.

She is gorgeous—there's no other word for her. Adorned in a traditional Yup'ik Alaskan parka lined with calf skins, fur, and a beaded chevron design ending at her solid thighs. The wind playfully ruffles the brown fur surrounding the hood, swirling her long black hair around her face. The traditional Yup'ik feminine line tattoo extends from her lips to her jaw, enhancing her natural beauty. Her voice scolding Trevor is the steady voice that safely guided us here.

"Mary, good to see you, too. When you gonna invite me to your hut?" Trevor laughs, winking at her.

My cheeks flush at his sexist and remarkably racist comments.

She dismisses him with a shake of her head and turns to me, a welcoming smile gracing her generous lips. "I'm Mary. Sorry for Trevor. I'm glad you're visiting us today. Welcome to my village, Portlock."

She holds out her hand, shaking mine firmly. Her warmth and strength flow through her handshake to my gloved hand. My body responds with heat zinging through me. Suddenly teary-eyed, I'm thankful to be alive and grateful to Mary for guiding us. Without her voice, I would've lost all hope, trapped in a small plane crashing into an unknown mountain. Knowing she was there, watching and guiding us, calmed me.

I'm unsure if the near-death experience caused my response or her startling beauty. Her warm eyes, stunning stature, and inner strength dazzle me. I can barely bring myself to release her hand and speak.

"Thank you, Mary. I'm the new nurse. I mean," I sputter, "I'm Riley, your new village nurse from the Alaska Community Health Program."

She smiles sincerely. "Yes, Riley. We don't get many visitors here. Go ahead and warm up." Mary points across the snow-swept lot to the Quonset hut. "I'll unload and have a talk with Trevor."

Her steady voice indicates she plans to gut him, and I'm not about to stop her.

Relieved to be alive and on solid ground, I nod my thanks, gather my binder, and walk to the building. The walk gives me time to contemplate my emotions—from the abject fear of crashing into a remote mountainside to my blossoming desire for my gorgeous Yup'ik rescuer, Mary.

"There's coffee and frybread inside," she calls out, then turns, berating Trevor in a low, gruff tone. She's talking too quietly for me to discern her words.

Whatever she's saying seems effective, as Trevor stares at his feet and mumbles, nodding in response. He kicks at the frost-covered gravel.

I hope she reports his hazardous flying to the FAA or his company. Heck, I hope she punches him, too.

Trudging inside, I realize my thin city jacket and professional office clothing are inadequate for the chilly fall weather. Thank goodness my warm winter clothing is in my luggage. I'll layer it on when I get it from my bag.

I didn't anticipate how cold it would be without a large heated airliner, modern airport, and indoor walkways. I'm already getting culture shock, and I've only just arrived.

Live and learn. This is my first village trip on my first week as a village nurse, my first nursing job. On the next trip, I'll wear my thermal underwear and snow jacket on the plane. And I'll fake sleeping to avoid unnecessary conversation.

Kathy hired me directly after I graduated. The Alaskan Community Health Program always needs nurses to visit remote villages. Villages have no medical care, and few nurses want to work in the Alaskan bush. She hired me by the end of the interview, from her Anchorage office. I will work in each village with my main work location based in an office in Anchorage, where I already live.

She told me that villagers must typically call for medical air support without nurses there, flying sick villagers to Anchorage for their medical needs. The remote villages should have a permanent nurse stationed in each village, but the program doesn't have the staff. Thus, the villagers get me instead—a traveling nurse providing flu shots.

When I completed my rotation at the Alaska Native Medical Center and saw the Alaskan villagers without basic medical care, I knew what I wanted to do. I passionately believe every person deserves and has the right to quality medical care. Immediately, I applied to work in remote villages, envisioning doing well-child clinics, tracking tuberculosis outbreaks, and saving villagers' lives. Instead, my first task is the mundane job of giving flu shots.

I'm not thwarted, though. I have a plan. If I prove that Portlock needs more care, and I can give that care, then I can do more interesting medical interventions, saving more lives. Soon, I will plan my trips to Portlock and choose the nursing interventions to help the village.

I figure that I need to vaccinate at least twenty-five people, which is ten percent of the village, to succeed in showing that I can do the job and the village wants my help. And building on my flu clinic success will prove to Kathy that I'm a good nurse and know what I'm doing.

Although a vaccination clinic is more paperwork than actually doing real medical work, protecting the villagers against influenza is an easy, needed intervention. Considering influenza still kills, notably in villages where flu spreads fast and there's no clinic or hospital here to give proper medical care, this isn't a worthless task-it's just boring.

Growing up in Anchorage, I completed Alaskan Studies in school. White explorers' historic decimation of villages by diseases such as influenza is a large part of Alaskan history. Not to mention, the explorers stripped the Inuit Peoples of natural resources. Without men to hunt, furs to trade, and fish to eat, the tribes couldn't survive as they did before. Justifiably, villagers are now wary of all outsiders.

Even twenty years ago, Portlock village elders met airplanes with rifles, preventing visitors from getting off planes and visiting their village. And who can blame them? If they refused the first visitors, their village population would be in the thousands, not the hundreds.

I'm glad the village welcomes me as the government tries to make amends and create programs to help. Smiling and hopeful, I'm proud to be a part of the future, respecting our Alaskan Inuit population and allowing them to thrive on their traditional lands.

Assessing the dark airport building, I imagine living here without a medical clinic, only two friends the same age as me, no grocery store, and no Starbucks. I can't imagine growing up here. Even the wildest survivalist shows don't film in the Arctic-it's too treacherous and not survivable. Imagining Inuit people: men, women, babies, elderly people living in this desolate place is beyond my comprehension. The unforgiving, harsh environment, with its biting cold and relentless snowstorms, starkly contrasts the familiar comforts of my urban upbringing. The isolation here is more than geographical. There's a detachment from the conveniences of modern life. In this challenging environment, the thought of children playing, elders sharing stories, and families enduring the harsh winters seems like fairytales.

I rub my frozen hands to get the blood flowing again. Then, I collapse on the comfy leather chair next to the coffee, a jar of blueberry jam, and frybread dusted with powdered sugar.

Kathy explained it takes years for the villagers and elders to accept outsiders into their village. She preemptively called the Portlock elders to introduce me and arrange this village trip. While she telephoned them from her office and left messages since villages don't usually use cell phones or email, I examined the village gifts in her office from smoked fish and pickled seal flippers. *The jar is labeled, or I'd have no clue what it was!* Also, a large bag of orange salmon berries, and jars upon jars of Alaskan jams are proudly displayed.

With Kathy's introduction and my Alaskan background, I'm hopeful the villagers will welcome me, too, despite being a white outsider. Maybe I'll bring home some village gifts from this trip. Hopefully, I'll receive jams *and not fermented seal flipper*, though.

Kathy last visited Portlock three years ago, but she tells me the airport traffic controller and school secretary are the village elders I need to win over. I plan to disarm them with my caring and enthusiasm. Then, I help as many villagers as possible with the flu vaccine and learn more about their village medical needs. After my successful visit, the villagers will know I'm more than an outside government official. I'm a caring nurse who wants to support their village.

I pour a cup of coffee, adding five spoonfuls of sugar. I *need* the caffeine and sugar to revive my nerves. I still have a full day of medical work.

Thinking about my busy day, I dial my mom before I'm too busy to chat. She wanted me to check in, and after such a harrowing ride, I need all the support I can get. Despite her feelings about village work's unpredictable and dangerous nature, she wants me to succeed. Of course, in the back of her mind, she'll secretly be rooting for me to be scared off and move to the safe hospital surgical nursing job she set up for me.

I did try a rotation in her surgical department, but being a doctor's handmaiden is not my dream. I want to advocate for health equity and heal social injustices. I'm a dreamer and a doer, and I'm doing more with my medical knowledge than blotting a surgeon's forehead.

My mom answers my call, and I update her, unloading my worries before putting on my professional nursing demeanor. As I talk, Mary returns, pushing a cart filled with the totes and supplies unloaded from the plane.

In the background, Trevor's bush plane roars away as I say goodbye to my mom.

I noticed that Mary didn't invite Trevor inside for coffee and frybread.

Good Riddance to him. I hope I don't see him again. But then I remember, I'm flying home with him this evening. *Ugh!*

As she approaches, her eyes catch mine, and there's a shared understanding in that glance, as if she senses my reluctance and how out of place I feel here. A subtle smile plays on her lips, reassuring me.

She parks the cart, and the warmth returns to the room from Mary's presence, not just from the heater kicking in after opening the door.

I wish my mom "goodbyes" and hang up to chat with Mary and ignore my discomfort of thinking about my return flight.

With a twinkle in her eye, she slides a plate of frybread my way. "You'll need this. Facing the Alaskan wilderness on an empty stomach isn't recommended."

I laugh, grateful for the distraction. "Thanks, Mary. I appreciate it."

My worries fade as I bite into the sweet frybread, and I'm ready for the challenge.

Chapter 3

Elder Mary

On the airfield, I reach out and grasp Nurse Riley's delicate fingers, I am grateful to hold her hand safely in mine while helping her off the aircraft. I sense her overwhelming relief at touching the solid earth again—a sensation I share.

Fucking Trevor and his hotdogging!

Riley is young and earnest, making me want to punch the dumbass for causing her blue eyes to be red-rimmed and wet with worry. Our village needs healthcare, and Trevor is terrorizing our new village nurse. She'll never visit us again with his flying antics.

I notice her tight smile and silent response to Trevor's flirting on the runway.

Oblivious to the tension, Trevor continues to lay on his boorish charm. I manage to put Riley at ease by suggesting she indulge in a coffee at the airport while I chat with Trevor one-on-one.

The arrangement saves Riley and allows me to convey a message to Trevor. Despite being a small village, I won't hesitate to take drastic measures if he persists in jeopardizing our villagers' safety and the timely delivery of our essential supplies.

I manage our airport and village. And I'm not about to let Trevor or anyone else disrespect our people. If he thinks he can skate by doing a shitty job, he's mistaken. Outsiders think we should be grateful for anything they provide, but I expect the same service a city would get—planes arriving on time, cargo delivered on time, and a capable pilot.

Poor Riley got stuck with our worst bush pilot. At least her visit to us can only get better after their near-crash landing.

Something about her sweet countenance, captivating blue eyes, and the subtle touch of her hand makes me feel protective. It reminds me of my first romantic relationship at the University of Anchorage's Aviation School.

My insides warm thinking back to the memories, I let the nostalgia of my first romance engulf me. With the chilly wind and a plane to unload, Riley's blue eyes spark my memory, transporting me to a different time and place.

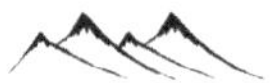

The crisp city air fills my nostrils, accompanied by the bustling symphony of urban life-car engines rumbling, appliances humming, and students chattering in the dormitories. I am woefully inexperienced at traveling outside my small village, and moving to the big city for my flight training is an exhilarating and terrifying new experience—Anchorage sprawls before me, vast and teeming with unfamiliar faces.

"I'm Aurora," my roommate says, with a crooked smile and blue eyes, as I wander into our room after being lost in the dormitory's maze for an hour.

Aurora is my first friend in the city. She was born and raised in Anchorage by a single mom. Thus, Aurora is fiercely independent and unafraid. Her ability to navigate the city and people, makes her worldly and sophisticated compared to me, who couldn't figure out how to use a busy crosswalk—push the button, then the light will change and you can walk across.

Taking my hand, Aurora becomes my guide to city life. Amidst the big city, I find solace in the bubble we create, hiding against the urban backdrop. She unveils Anchorage's wonders, sneaking me into bars, strolling hand-in-hand through the campus commons, and exploring the serene, snow-covered moonlight parks.

Gone are the lonely, quiet village days, transforming into busy city days. My university life is a blizzard of discovery and adventure—falling in love included.

I fall hard for Aurora, and our intense first love makes me physically sick, excited, hot, and unable to stand still or keep moving. My mind is calm and stormy. Loving Aurora opens a passion inside me I never fathomed.

No longer am I an outsider, a hunter, or a Yup'ik girl who stands apart. When I'm with Aurora, I am simply me, and she is Aurora. We are inseparable, our fingers perpetually entwined, laughter becoming the soundtrack to exploring the city and each other.

Even at home in my village, surrounded by my family and supportive community, I didn't quite fit in. I was isolated, watching my friends date and start families. With Aurora, I fit. I belong. And I am not alone.

Now, I understand why I never found *my person*, my love. It wasn't me being different but more so I didn't have anyone similar to myself in the village. I do possess a passionate and loving side, which Aurora revealed. She activates my hidden DNA turnings on my romantic nature—a yearning and hunger living inside me. My passion grows, only quenched by her laugh, hands, and taste.

Our lips fit perfectly, and we tenderly explore each other on our university weekends. We haven't experienced love before—we allow our new intimacy to unfold without questioning or defining it.

Being with Aurora introduces me to a vibrant unknown world beyond flight training and uncovers a missing piece of my identity. I realize who I am—an assertive and passionate individual capable of wholehearted love and a loving relationship. My strangeness growing up finally makes sense... why my male village friends flirting never stirred my attraction, why my heart skips a beat whenever Aurora smiles at me, and why kissing a village boy feels unnatural, but her lips fit mine perfectly.

There's much more than flight training to learn in Anchorage. In the city, I meet strangers and have experiences I couldn't have experienced in my comfortable little village.

Loving a woman is a non-traditional path, which is perfectly okay because my attraction to females is undeniably my path. Aurora's openness, blue eyes, and unwavering acceptance lead me. I embrace being a strong Yup'ik person *and* a passionate woman.

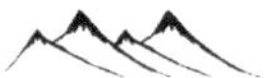

As my memories dissipate, I enjoy the lingering emotional echoes, intensified by my encounter with the blue-eyed city nurse. The warmth of my brief, intense affair with Aurora pulses through my body, and I shake my head to clear my mind. I return to the task on the cold runway.

I must focus on the current task—unloading the cargo—that Trevor conveniently neglected to assist me with. I unpack and lash down the cargo into my old Bronco truck, ready to seek shelter from the biting cold and speak more with our visitor.

True to form, Trevor fulfills the bare minimum of his duties by delivering the village mail and the passenger. But he conveniently sidesteps unloading the cargo or extending any welcoming gesture to me. His outsider attitude and lack of professionalism are disheartening—really, his shortcomings of not being a decent human being is appalling.

The situation is tricky, though. If I voice my concerns and file a report with the FAA regarding his dangerous flying, Trevor might get fired. His actions would leave our village without a scheduled cargo delivery until they find a replacement. And who's to say the next outsider they hire won't be *even worse* than Trevor?

Trevor barges into our village without seeking permission, disrespects our land and People, and ignores my advice. However, he does arrive and delivers our cargo five days a week.

I warned Trevor to slow down, be mindful, and respect the land by flying high over Portlock. I caution all the pilots about our ancestors' spirits, who whisper in the wind, nudging planes dangerously close to the river's edge and the mountain's snowy peaks. Our mountains draw outsiders to them, forcing planes to fly too close.

But time and time again, pilots brush aside my warnings, disregarding my experience and credentials. They dismiss me as nothing more than "a superstitious villager" or "a silly woman".

Yet, when Riley stepped off the plane, her sensitive blue eyes fixated on our village landscape, there was something different about her—a respect glimmering in her gaze, a recognition of the beauty and power surrounding us. *And damn, those eyes are attractive - undeniably so.*

I haven't encountered an outsider in Portlock who captivates me like Riley. Her soft smile and those eyes are hypnotic, causing my breath to quicken. I climb into the Bronco, making my way into the hangar. She's awakened my dormant feminine passion, filling me with youth and excitement like my university days with Aurora.

What am I thinking? I refocus on unloading the cargo.

After all, *I am a respected Portlock Village Elder,* representing our village and tribe. I instill our sacred traditions and culture to our village children and teach our culture to outsiders. I make essential village decisions and sit on village councils to protect our Yup'ik ways. By welcoming outsiders, I ensure they do not harm our village or People.

No matter how breathtaking the city outsider is, I cannot allow myself to be distracted from my duties to our People—especially by a beautiful, city outsider!

My focus must remain on my village.

Chapter 4

Elder Mary

Walking into Portlock's airport hangar, I overhear the nurse talking on her cell phone while rocking back in my leather chair.

I hope her cell phone data plan is top-notch, as there are no cell towers in Portlock. I should warn her about the huge data use costs of cell phone calls in Portlock, but I'll let the city girl figure it out.

Today, Riley is learning about the village culture, people, and background. Teaching her how to make a call in a remote village is not my priority. Riley must understand our Yup'ik culture and meet the Portlock village elders.

"Mom, I almost died! This place is dark and cold—my nose hair is frozen, and my eyeballs ache..." Riley pauses, presumably listening to her mom talk. She smears her pink lip gloss on the mug's rim while she sips coffee.

She is entirely oblivious to my entrance. She's not from the village—the cell phone glued to her ear, the pink lip gloss, the flimsy lightweight jacket offering no protection from the cold, her blond hair intricately styled in an elaborate braid, and wearing her white button-up shirt paired with black slacks, and athletic shoes.

I will teach the outsider about Alaskan village life's intricacies during her day visit. To survive this harsh wilderness, we bundle ourselves in warm parkas and don layers of woolen clothing. Makeup and hairstyling are not a priority, as our faces remain covered by balaclavas and our hair tucked securely under hats. Riley stands out—an exotic peacock amidst our fur-lined arctic coverings—with her pink Gore-Tex jacket.

Why can't the government send us individuals who genuinely understand village life and our rich culture instead of thrusting these city outsiders upon us?

"No," Riley responds to her mother. "It's so remote. The only way to reach here is by bush plane. And he's the only pilot available. I'm sure I'm being overdramatic, and he'll be fine flying me home..."

As I clank the cargo, unloading it onto the table, I smile, appreciating her optimism. I hope our fall weather doesn't take a turn for the worse; otherwise, she'll find herself snowed in, trapped in Portlock until a plane can safely land. She wouldn't last a day in our rugged little village. With her fair hair and delicate frame, she is more a Barbie doll than an Alaskan wilderness nurse.

However, looks can be deceiving, and I loathe outsiders stereotyping me as a *Butch Wilderness Native.* I won't assume she is weak or judge her. I'll give this soft, beautiful city girl the benefit of the doubt and believe she's tougher than she appears. I'm sure Riley is capable of surviving Alaska's unforgiving wilderness, or she wouldn't have accepted a village nursing position.

At least, I hope so—for her sake.

"Maybe," Riley continues, then responds, "This is why I became a village nurse, and it's what I want to do with my life." She looks, seeing me watching her, and realizes I am waiting for her.

"Sorry, Mom. I need to go," she hastily says, then ends her call.

"I apologize for the interruption," I say, offering a warm smile. "I hope you enjoyed the coffee and frybread. They're the best in Portlock."

"I do. Thank you. Honestly, I needed the caffeine," Riley says with a nervous laugh and sips the coffee.

I continue my warm smile, determined to fulfill my role as the official village welcome party.

"Let me extend our village's welcome and gratitude for your visit." I declare, gesturing towards the freshly brewed coffee and homemade frybread I prepared earlier.

Living in Portlock, I wear many hats, and welcoming outsiders to our village is one of the most important. After greeting visitors, I accompany them throughout the village and ensure our culture is understood and respected.

Part of my welcoming includes sizing up the outsiders to protect our village if I find they are not here for our benefit. This summer, a land management company arrived to map our tundra areas, but I figured out their true objective was to find and extract natural gas.

With this information, the village elders promptly escorted them back to their plane and firmly explained they were not welcome in our village. We fiercely protect our resources and cultural heritage. Outsiders will no longer be exploiting us or our land.

We have endured losing our traditions, people, and resources to outsiders' influences. Hence, we approach visitors with caution, even when they claim noble intentions. By managing the airport and offering transportation, I maintain a vigilant watch over those who enter our village. I won't allow any trouble into our community.

"The coffee and donuts are absolutely delicious," Riley says, biting into a fluffy, powdered-sugared delicacy.

I cringe as she rebrands our traditional frybread as a "donut".

Will she be calling me an Indian next? Or perhaps she will ask for a dogsled ride to visit the village clinic housed in an igloo.

I grit my teeth, resigning to yet another encounter with a well-meaning white government outsider who fails to grasp our Yup'ik traditions and stories. They come here, thinking they are "helping" our community, imposing their ideas without understanding our history and needs.

Instead of consulting the village elders and seeking our input on what the village requires, the government continues disregarding our people, imposing their foreign decisions onto us. They tell us what we are "eligible" to receive. They need to realize direct funding to our village council would allow us to allocate resources appropriately and be far more beneficial. I hoped Riley was different.

Riley turns around, her words tumbling out. "I thought a village elder was going to welcome me today?"

I force a smile, masking the deepening grimace at her ongoing cultural offenses.

Riley is culturally clueless despite being our village nurse.

I am the village elder, standing before her, representing our community's wisdom and traditions. *I am the one who is welcoming her to our village.*

Chapter 5

Elder Mary

I shake my head, giving Riley a patient smile. "Age and gender don't define a village elder. They aren't simply old Inuit men," I explain. "An elder is a respected tribe member who oversees and represents the community. I proudly represent our village on the Alaska Council in Anchorage while leading Portlock youth and managing the airport."

With a graceful motion, I shrug off the red fancy parka I wore, especially for Riley's visit. The garment itself is a living testament to our village's heritage. Every intricate glass bead which adorns its surface tells a story passed down from generation to generation. My grandmother taught me the art of beading over long winter nights around the fire. Our talented young villager, Ellen, meticulously sewed the fur lining, proudly showcasing last year's hunting bounty featuring beaver and wolverine fur. We prize both animals for their meat, warm fur, and vital spirits, which reincarnated, blessing us next season.

Nevertheless, my heart sinks with my self-reproach. *How could I assume a city outsider would notice or appreciate these intricate details, let alone inquire about the stories woven within them?*

An apologetic flush colors Riley's cheeks as she murmurs, "Oh, I'm sorry. I didn't realize." She quickly adds, "Thank you for the coffee."

I offer a gentle nod, acknowledging her apology and gratitude.

Her gaze falls upon the table, and she eagerly asks, "Can I lend a hand with unloading?"

My face softens at her willingness to help and learn. "Yes, in a moment. I'll enjoy a coffee then you can tour Portlock, as I deliver mail and escort you to the clinic."

Her brows furrow in concern. "Shouldn't I head to the clinic first? I don't want to be late." Her clipped comment reveals her city, outsider culture as she rudely glances at her watch.

I shake my head at this. *There's not enough time to explain the village's rhythm, which isn't based on a clock but moves gently to nature's beat.*

"There is time," I assure her, calm and confident. I understand there is no rush, and the village is waiting to meet the new nurse when she's ready, not at an appointed time.

Pouring myself steaming coffee, I settle beside Riley, savoring the warmth radiating through the ceramic mug. A companionable silence descends upon us, allowing the gentle symphony of the wind to weave its music. I imagine her enjoying the village's tranquil silence, a dramatic difference from the city's frantic loudness.

Riley fidgets slightly, discomfort written on her features. The cold air finds her through the building's cracks, whispering secrets as the small heater in the corner valiantly fights against the biting cold to maintain a comfortable temperature inside.

Her pink jacket remains on, and she sits with her empty coffee mug. She fills the silence rather than be in it.

"I'm Nurse Riley," she says, her voice filling the space between us, despite already introducing herself on the airfield and in her emailed announcement to the village elders regarding her visit. She continues aimlessly chatting, offering conversational tidbits about the weather, coffee, and upcoming clinic.

Lost in the winds mesmerizing ebb and flow, my attention drifts, catching only a few of her fragmented words. We'll enjoy a cooler night; perhaps our spirits will dance, splashing colors across the black sky, the aurora borealis or Northern Lights, as outsiders call them.

Without the gusting wind, the school children will explore outdoors, and villagers can travel by boat to fetch gas and groceries from the nearby larger Northern village, which unlike us, is large enough to support a grocery store and gas station. Taking a boat for groceries is much less expensive than taking a plane.

I pour the chatty nurse more coffee and smear my summer blueberry preserves on a "donut" for her. When I'm not working at the airport or flying my trusty little plane to hidden salmon streams, I spend my time hiking, hunting, picking, and canning berries—immersing myself in our land's bountiful offerings.

Comprehending our harmonious lifestyle is challenging for someone unaccustomed to village life. Our cultures' simplicity is profoundly beautiful, and our cherished traditions shape Portlock's unique character, fostering a tight-knit community. Each person respects and genuinely cares for their neighbors. Any villager is welcome into any home unannounced for dinner or a visit. I am fiercely proud and treasure our community's belonging and interconnectedness.

Embedded within our village's core values is our unwavering connection to nature. Unlike the city, which ignores or fights against the natural world, we embrace it. Nature envelops us, dictating our community's rhythms—be it the salmon season, berry-picking season, or hunting season. The wind carries our land's whispers, while the awe-inspiring scenery is a constant reminder of our ancestor's spirits.

As Riley pauses her chattering to savor her frybread, I seize the opportunity to offer guidance to help her comprehend our village's culture. I gesture toward the blueberry jam I crafted after a fruitful summer of berry-picking. Sharing jam is a gesture of sharing the earth's bounty and expressing gratitude.

"Riley, this is my homemade blueberry jam - shared with you to appreciate our land's offering. When you are offered fish or preserves, accept them. We take pride in our village, and sharing our land's abundance is a vital part of who we are."

Her eyes widen, and she eagerly bites into the frybread I pass her. "Thank you," she says, a blush gracing her cheeks. "I truly appreciate the food and the opportunity to learn about your village. And about you. I must confess, I tend to talk too much when I'm nervous and the plane ride shook me."

"Trevor should not fly between our mountains. The wind there is unpredictable. I warned him, but he ignored me. I am glad he regained control and you arrived safely," I remark.

She nods. "I need to start my clinic. Can you take me to the school on your way to the post office?"

I shake my head gently, regret crossing my face. The urgency in her demeanor leaves little room for her to enjoy our village's tranquil beauty and landscape. *Also, why do outsiders ignore learning about our village's stories and culture? Visitors don't ask me about my family, the weather, the fish running in the river, or the village traditions.*

Instead, Riley is like every other outsider who visits and is in a hurry to do whatever is on her to-do list and leave to return home to the city. She will finish her task, maybe take pictures, and leave here without actually understanding our village lifestyle and People.

Why isn't Riley different? I want her to care about us, to ask questions, and to hear our stories.

Her white skin, blond hair, and blue eyes contrast my natural Alaskan appearance, as her continued aimless chatter and inability to enjoy silence mark her as a city person. *What did I expect?*

I want to explain the difference between village seasons and city time. *How do I explain we ride the seasons and watch the tides?* There's no rush here, except when the salmon funnel through the river to the ocean. We rush to meet them and fill our freezers and smokers with a bounty that will last us the year.

Clocks are unnecessary in the village. School starts when you arrive, and dinner is when you are hungry. We keep a slower pace than city life, in sync with nature. *There's no way to explain village life to someone who's not experienced it.*

I start separating the mail. *The sooner I get Riley loaded into my truck and show her the village, the sooner she leaves. Then I will enjoy the day and tonight's northern lights.*

The now silent nurse finishes her coffee and frybread. She helps unload totes onto the table.

Although, when Riley's not talking, she is rather pleasant.

"Wait!" She pushes the mail aside, noticing the empty cart. Riley wrings her hands and begins breathing rapidly.

Are her hands shaking? Is she having a panic attack? I start, "Are you—"

"Where are my bags?" Riley's trembling voice cuts me off as her concerned eyes scan the cargo, growing wider with each passing second.

A chilling realization settles over me as her question hangs in the air.

Fucking Feckless Trevor!

Chapter 6

Nurse Riley

"This is everything." Mary's words echo in my ears, offering no comfort.

Panic surges through me as I realize the situation's gravity. My hands instinctively clutch at my chest to slow my racing heart.

"No!" I gasp, my voice wobbling, as I turn to Mary. "Where are the bags with my medical cooler and flu vaccines?"

"Not here." Her calm response is a hammer blow, instantly shattering my hopes.

As Mary's words fade into the background, my mind spins with the devastating consequences - my entire short nursing career flashes before my eyes. My aspirations and carefully crafted plans are ruined. I envisioned flying to remote Inuit villages, delivering life-saving care to grateful villagers, and rising through the ranks to become the youngest Alaska Community Medical Health Director. But, my dreams lie shattered, broken by my carelessness in losing the vital medical supplies essential for my job.

I'm ruined!

My mistake crashes over me, threatening to crumble my resolve. The vaccine's transportation and management is my sole purpose here in Portlock, and in less than an hour, I failed catastrophically.

I've lost the vaccines!

Poor Kathy will be forced to fire me for losing thousands of dollars in medical supplies and ruining the flu clinic.

Dread engulfs me, and I sink back into the leather chair before my legs buckle. I tell myself, *Stop freaking out*! But my heart is racing, and my mind is following it, running over every terrible scenario.

First, this village will be hit with a terrible influenza outbreak. Then the villagers will die of preventable diseases in record numbers, which will be my fault. Finally, the State will fire me and revoke my nursing license. I'll never work as a nurse again. And unable to pay back my student loans, I'll be in financial ruin living on Anchorage's streets, panhandling at traffic lights.

The chair rattles from my shaking, and tears wet my cheeks. My breathing is catching, and I'm woozy. I feel faint.

Mary settles beside me on the oversized chair's arm, her hand finding its place on my shoulder. "Take a slow breath in," she instructs gently. "1-2-3. And out. 1-2-3. Good! Breathe with me."

Like a child, I lay my head on her chest, my body curling into her solid body. Mary's calm voice is my lifeline, her soothing words guiding me through my panic attack as she tenderly strokes my back.

And then, with her soothing voice, she begins to talk, telling me a story. My mind slows, my focus solely on her words, as my heart and breathing align with her storytelling rhythm.

"My mom used to tell me the story of Two Old Women, a village legend that happened many moons ago," she begins, her voice steeped in tradition and wisdom.

On the chair, breathing in harmony with her, I inhale her musky, sweet scent reminding me of campfires and sugary frybread. I'm not a cuddler, and I can't remember the last time someone, aside from my mother, held me. With Mary's help, I'm relaxing and calm.

"Long ago as winter approached, our village had to migrate to survive by following the herds North. The villagers chose to leave two weaker elder grandmothers behind in the snowy wilderness while the village journeyed across the land to find food and shelter. The community believed the two weak old women would only slow them down and by leaving them behind, they would move faster and pull through before winter descended. With meager supplies and final farewells, the village left the old women alone, in the wilderness. However, the women resolved not to succumb to death but to live. They made a fire, hunted, and entertained each other. The elders were strong, not weak, and when spring came and they crossed the tundra to be reunited with their tribe, they found themselves stronger and healthier than their frail village. Their people were so weak, they could not hunt and were barely alive. The women forgave their tribe and saved them by imparting their wisdom and culture so they too, could survive."

Mary pauses, allowing the story's essence to settle around me.

My breath steadies, and I ask her, "Is it a true story?"

"Yes," Mary affirms, her gaze gentle yet resolute. "It is my people's story, a resilient community tested by hardships, from alcoholism to epidemics. We are not defined by weakness or our perceived inability to survive. Instead, we draw strength from our stories, our connections, and our ancestor's legacy. We thrive against all odds."

Mary's tender eyes warm me. "This story carries me through difficulties. Just like the old women, I will not be underestimated. These brave ancestors' blood is in my veins."

I sit up, a bit embarrassed, but I feel a connection with Mary, and my panic attack is fading. Mary's story calms my spirit, and her tenderness fuels a flame within me.

I am neither old nor weak, but I was succumbing to failure. The Yup'ik tale reminds me that I, too, am resilient. I am strong. And I'm not alone. Mary is with me, and she believes in me.

"What should I do?" I ask Mary.

"You do what you can," Mary says, her voice infused with confidence. "You give your best and trust that it is enough. I will locate Trevor, and my brother, Gary, will contact the nearby villages to find your supplies. We will find your vaccines.

"Okay." I nod, grateful for her support. My body is still warm from her holding me. I settle into that warmth, not wanting her heat to disappear.

Mary, a young woman, may not fit the Elder role I envisioned when arriving in Portlock. Even so, she embodies the wisdom, respect, and calming presence I hoped to experience when meeting a respected elder. She generously shared her village's oral history, unveiling an undeniably wisdom and peacefulness within her. We connected, and I succeeded in meeting and winning over one of the elders here.

"I will finish this and then introduce you to Portlock," Mary says.

"Okay. I'm going to update my boss. Then I'd love to tour Portlock," I declare, sitting taller, a renewed purpose flowing through my veins.

Before she rises, Mary offers a comforting hand on my arm. She leans in, and for a moment, I think she's going to kiss me.

I lean closer, ready to embrace her sweet, tender kiss.

But instead, she whispers in my ear, reassuring me, "You're going to be fine, Riley." She leans down, giving me a quick, warm hug.

Inhaling her sweet scent and feeling her warm breath on my sensitive neck ignites an emotional flurry in my chest. I forget my fear and failure in her arms.

Mary takes a small step back, and the intimate moment dissipates without a kiss.

Surprisingly, my heart is disappointed. I zip up my jacket, looking forward to her escorting me throughout the village.

Chapter 7

Elder Mary

I look up from calling my brother, the Portlock School Principal, as Riley wipes away her tears, still wet on her cheeks.

These city creatures are rather fragile. Although, to be fair, Trevor attempted to kill her with his careless flying, and now she can't robotically follow her vaccination clinic schedule.

Despite presenting as a woman, I am not comfortable with her crying. Living in the village, I've experienced crying only a handful of times; we share and accept our emotions. For villagers, we don't harbor problems more significant than what an auntie, uncle, or elder can help solve or carry for us. No tears are needed here.

Oddly, I want to embrace her again. I want her tender body pressed against my heart and the feeling from our hug as my lips whisper against her neck.

Rather than embrace her, I step back and wait for her to be ready.

"Since I can't do my clinic without vaccines. I ruined this entire trip! I'm responsible for managing them and this trip I'm supposed to prove myself to Kathy and the Alaska Community Medical Program. They never hire new, right-out-of-nursing-school nurses. And I need to show my mom that I can hack it as a village nurse."

She says this quickly in one breath. Her eyes fill with emotion, and glossy tears form at her lashes as she explains her swirling feelings.

"I'm going to get fired. That's thousands of dollars in vaccinations I've lost and a waste trip here. They'll be thawed by the time Trevor comes back tonight and unusable."

Instinctively, I tenderly embrace her, my arm hovering protectively around her as if I can shield her from her worries.

Work is Riley's only priority. *How stressful for her entire identity to be tied to her work without a community to help her.*

"Riley, my brother will track down your vaccines. He has contacts in the neighboring villages. Until then, you will enjoy a village tour, and the kids at the school have been calling me all morning, waiting to meet you."

"I hope I don't disappoint them, too," Riley says, sniffing.

"Impossible," I say encouragingly.

She is less defeated but still lost, looking at her watch, counting down the time to return home from the

Alaskan Bush to civilization. I want her to see and love my village, but that is impossible.

"Adapting to the situation is part of living in a village. Let's make the most of you being here. I'll take you on the official village tour, meet the villagers, and you can inspire our future generation. We have a student who wants to be a nurse," I explain, hoping to buoy her spirit.

"Okay," she says reluctantly, pulling at her jacket.

"Come to the post office with me. And then, I'll take you to the school and show you our little clinic," I say, talking more than usual as I try to comfort her.

"Yes. I might as well," Riley says, erasing the frown with a smile and nodding.

"Bob. Bob. When are you going to bring over the nurse?" The CB radio screeches at us, breaking the silence.

I pick up the radio to silence it.

"Gary, I am heading there after the Post Office. Can you call your village phone tree and find Trevor? He didn't unload the nurse's flu vaccines and supplies."

"Gotcha. Stop by the school for lunch, we've made salmon chowder special and I'll locate the medical supplies, no problem," my brother's confident voice responds.

I click the radio back in response. After hearing Gary's confidence in finding Trevor and her medical supplies, Riley glows with newfound assurance. I hope she will enjoy seeing our little community now.

"It's not terrible, Cheechako. You get to relax before working," I tell her with a smile.

She frowns at "cheechako," taking offense. In the village, we call all outsiders "cheechako". I might need to amend my habit; no one enjoys being labeled or stereotyped. I strive to be open-minded and honor individuals. *Why am I so quick to judge Riley?*

"I am an Alaskan, born and raised here. I might enjoy Starbucks and drive a Prius, but I'm no Cheechako," she says, lifting her chin.

"I apologize. I lived in Anchorage for years, and yes, Anchorage is still Alaska. Forgive me?" I ask with my hands raised in peace.

At least she's motivated, with a fire in her belly again.

As we walk out the door, she surveys the land. I imagine her thoughts as she judges our snowy village, dusk's darkness lingering at ten o'clock. Portlock is no city. There are no restaurants or shops here. Our most prominent building is the school and we rely on the land to provide and the planes to deliver necessities.

She stares at the unpaved dirt road leading into the village with its one lane, since that's all we need here. Portlock is a land island trapped by mountains with the harsh tundra isolating us. The only way into Portlock is to travel by airplane or boat when the river is thawed.

"Welcome to the Bush," I tell her, walking to my truck, carrying the last mail tote to load.

"Thank you. Portlock is quiet," Riley responds, pausing, her breath making a white halo cloud around her.

"Riley?" I ask, opening the door for her.

"Coming," she says, shaking her head at the landscape and climbing into my old Bronco.

Chapter 8

Nurse Riley

I shiver, gazing out over the Alaskan's cold, desolate tundra. The snow-capped mountains gleam in the morning light, and the vast empty wilderness stretches for miles ahead. The dark landscape is radically different from my home, Anchorage. I'm an alien intruding on another planet.

To these villagers, I am an outsider, a "cheechako" from the city. I want to disprove their bias. *But how do I show them I'm a caring nurse when I can't even give them the planned flu vaccinations?*

I wrap my jacket tighter around myself for warmth - failing miserably as the cold sinks into my bones. My coat isn't protecting me from Portlock's icy weather. My chill is as much from the cold sinking into me as the isolation and loneliness in the desolate landscape.

The cold barrenness stretches on for miles in every direction, with no lights to indicate habitation and not a single building sticking out from the snow.

Mary calls me to her truck, and I gratefully sit in the warm Bronco as we drive the icy road to the village.

From my research, this single dirt road leads from the airport, winds through the village, and ends at the school, which houses the medical clinic.

How depressing, one dirt road and no Starbucks!

Mary is unfazed by the dreary landscape. "This is the post office and beyond it is the main village with the school and our clinic," she explains, stopping at a metal structure labeled "Portlock Post Office."

"Super," I say.

I wrap myself tighter in my jacket as I trudge into the tiny post office, the first building in town.

The Portlock Post Office is bright and warm, and I smile, soaking in the normalness. The halogen lights, metal mailboxes, outgoing mail slot, and big mail counter are the same as any post office in Anchorage.

After the long counter and scales, a community bulletin board announces a rifle for sale, and someone needs a ride (on a boat presumably) to the next town for their much-needed pepperoni hot pockets.

A teenager, perhaps?

"Hey Bob!" The man behind the counter waves to greet Mary.

"Frank, this is Nurse Riley," Mary gestures to me, and I offer a little wave back.

Mary turns to me. "We will be at the post office for the next hour. Since the plane came in, everyone will be coming to collect their mail. And you will meet every household in Portlock. Then I will take you to the school and clinic."

This is the most she's said to me since telling me the Old Women story. I nod, thinking, *An hour? Who spends an hour at a post office?*

"Our Postmaster, Frank, is Portlock's social mayor," Mary explains.

Frank grins at the mayor's title introduction. "The village elder council thinks they run this place." Frank winks at me. "The post office is the most happening place in town. Everyone comes here for their groceries and mail. And I have the city news and the local gossip." He pins the latest Anchorage Daily Newspaper to the Community Board next to the request for pizza pockets.

"Ding. Ding." The bell above the entrance rings as villagers stream in to collect their mail as Mary unloads on the counter while Frank sorts it.

I step aside, noticing the vast Amazon boxes filled with snacks, soda, and laundry soap. *How weird getting your groceries by mail!*

Mary's right about this being the social hub as the villagers rush into the Post Office, wrapped in furry parkas against the chill, and nod their greetings to each other.

The Postmaster hands out the mail without needing to announce names or having a lineup of customers.

I stand in the corner and pull out my phone, taking advantage of the distraction to start my to-do list for returning from this trip. I will officially apologize to my manager for the vaccine debacle. And if Kathy doesn't fire me, I need to book another village visit to give the flu vaccines. Then I will go grocery shopping and schedule dinner with my mom to discuss her hospital connections, just in case I need to start job hunting again.

As I'm fixated on my phone's tiny screen, tapping away at my to-do list, I hear grumbling to Mary about "another white nurse" and how they haven't sent the "big mail plane yet". What I gather from the comments is that a bigger plane will bring someone's new table, another's microwave, and a mattress, which doesn't fit into the small bush plane delivery.

Mary nods in response and points me out to the villagers waiting for their mail.

"Riley, come meet my people," Mary encourages, coming beside me, nudging me away from my phone.

I pocket my phone, smile and shake the villagers' hands, nodding at their greetings and valiantly trying to remember names.

"Well, at least Stacy is excited to meet you. She's waiting to meet you at the school," Margot comments after being introduced to me.

Mary explains, "Stacy is her daughter. She is enrolled in the University of Anchorage's nursing school next year. She wants to be our permanent village nurse."

"Of course," I say, hoping she's friendlier than her mother.

"Stacy is really excited about your visit and asking questions about nursing school. A nurse visit is rare these last years, and she wanted to talk with one ever since she applied and won the nursing scholarship for the University of Anchorage," Margot adds.

"I'll be happy to meet and talk with her. I graduated from UA," I say, wondering if Stacy will adapt to Anchorage. Anchorage is drastically different from the village, and she will need to adjust to the crush of city people, paved highways with traffic lights, and the grueling nursing program's schedule.

Mary next introduces me to Elder Rena, who manages the school's food pantry and cafeteria.

Rena explains, "I keep the basics in the school emergency pantry – rice, spam, sailor bread, sugar, salt, and such. Then if anyone runs out of supplies before the next plane, they can get what they need."

"Does the state give you any grant money for your program?" I ask.

"No. I stock it and people restock it when they go shopping or if they have extra food. I'm heading back and I'll see you there."

I note on my phone: *Research the government food insecurity grant and apply for it to assist the Portlock Emergency pantry managed by Elder Rena.* I see Mary frowning at my phone, and I slip it back into my pocket.

I slowly meet the entire town, including Pete, the local Village Safety Officer, who takes on the role of policing the village. He is also the primary employer with the fish processing plant at the river's edge.

Since Mary's from Portlock, making the introductions is easy for her. The only villagers not here are the school-aged children and the principal/teacher, Gary.

Mary respectfully nods, greeting each person and sharing a few words before smoothly transitioning to introducing me. Strangely, people continue to call her "Bob".

I want to ask her about everyone calling her Bob, but there's no pause between her introductions. Before I can ask, a villager approaches.

"This is Elder Harold," Mary introduces.

"Don't bother, Bob," Harold says. "Why should I remember a new name when you'll only be here one or two more times before you decide our village isn't *for you*?"

I'm offended, and perhaps this explains why people are only half-heartedly greeting me and learning my name. The villagers assume I'm another outsider, visiting them once without plans to return or learn their names.

"Hello, Harold. It's nice to meet you. I'm your new village nurse, and I *am an Alaskan,* born and raised. *I am coming back* to provide whatever care you need. What do you suggest I do in the village?"

"We need a dentist. I cracked a tooth, and there are families who haven't seen a dentist in over ten years," he says promptly.

"I will definitely talk to the dental program about sending a dentist here. I'll check the clinic today and assess what dental tools we have to let them know your needs," I further explain.

I'm glad he actually answers me and explains his health needs. Dental care in the village is vital, and although cleaning teeth is a menial task, excellent oral care is a crucial preventative health intervention. I'll add this information to my village report to follow up with when I return home.

After Harold walks away, grumbling at my response, Mary asks, "How long do you plan to be a government village nurse?"

Even Mary thinks I will be scared off by village work and leaving the position.

"I chose to work in the villages because I want to help fellow Alaskans who don't have access to medical care. I'm an Alaskan and the villages don't scare me. I'm staying for the long haul," I say. "Well, unless I get fired for losing those vaccines," I add quietly, remembering my fate remains undetermined.

"Let's go visit Gary at the school. I am sure he's found them," Mary says, patting my back encouragingly.

She is a superb tour guide and helps distract me from my disastrous trip. I'm glad she encourages me to make the best of my Portlock visit and tour the village with her.

If not, I'd be pouting about my lost vaccines at the airport. And my shoulder and stomach wouldn't tingle with excitement at her touch.

Meeting the villagers is invigorating, and I'm starting to understand the community. *How strange it is to be familiar with every villager and each day to be predictably the same and the highlight being a "big plane delivery"?*

"Thank you for introducing me, and showing me around," I tell Mary.

"My job is introducing you to our community," she responds, "and I am happy to do it. I'm enjoying spending time with you."

My heart warms at her simple statement. I enjoy her easy smile and laid-back attitude, too. I could stare at her lustrous black hair and traditional tattoo for hours. She is a beautiful person both inside and outside.

The post office visit is a nice distraction from my planned flu clinic, and despite my sour mood at Trevor, I'm happy to meet the villagers.

Mary meets my eyes and smiles, "Let's head to the school. You can tour the clinic area, and we'll talk to Gary."

I nod in agreement. I pray, *Please, Gary, tell me you've found my missing medical supplies. Then I can complete my flu clinic, and my job is safe.*

Chapter 9

Nurse Riley

A flash in the dark snowy tundra catches my eye as we drive on the dirt track to the opposite side of town to Portlock's school. We've already passed the houses and the villagers walking home with their mail.

"Stop!" I yell to Mary.

Mary slams the brakes, and the truck lurches, skidding to a halt. She turns her head, looking for an obstacle.

"I see . . .saw. . .something. . ." I start. But I can't explain the weird flash or my gut feeling that we needed to stop.

I open the truck's door and hop out before Mary asks any questions because I honestly can't explain. *Something isn't right.*

She leaves the truck running, the headlights illuminate the isolated tundra, and opens her door, silently following me out into the darkness. The Alaskan morning lingering darkness blankets the landscape as the late-rising sun paints the sky with a deep blue and soft purple, creating a mysterious atmosphere.

"There!" I say more to myself as another reflection flashes in front of us. I start walking to where the elusive reflection came from, the mysterious object in the tundra catching my attention.

Mary's boots crunch behind my already-cold feet as I shuffle with the snow falling into my thin running shoes, the blanketed snowy ground annoyingly just above my shoe level.

I packed snow boots and a thicker jacket in my bag, but they are who-knows-where flying around the Alaskan bush with that asshole pilot Trevor.

Did he purposely forget to unload my bags since I didn't swoon at his offer for a date?

The silvery white flash beckons again three feet to my right. The flash comes with a scurrying sound making my skin crawl.

I loathe rats, lizards, spiders, and everything which scurries. *But rats don't live in the tundra, right?* No dirty rats and snakes are a definite advantage to living here.

My feet carry me to the sound and the last reflection on the side of the snowy road.

"What is that?" Mary asks with a puzzled voice.

Good! At least I'm not crazy since an experienced elder also sees the flashing and hears the noise. And Mary can't identify it, either.

From my calculations, a mysterious tundra robot rat is an unusual situation and maybe an emergency.

My gut tells me someone – or something– is in trouble, which propels me forward, giving me the confidence to approach the alien noise.

Do Alaska Inuit People experience alien encounters? Do aliens visit the desolate villages?

A small, dark furry body with an oversized shaking glass head appears in the icy ditch.

My hand darts and catches the creature before my brain processes the danger.

"Wait!" Mary says with urgency.

"Sorry," I shrug, turning to her and into the headlights to reveal my captive.

I'm holding a scrawny feral cat with a mini jiffy peanut butter jar stuck on her head. Her head is much too large for this little jar. I can only make out dark fur without features inside the container, even with her face wedged inside the glass.

The cat's dehydration is evident by her limp body and unusually sluggish movements. Even in my hands, she is shaking her head and lifting her paw, weakly knocking at it.

I'd bet she's endured her head stuck inside the jar for days and lacks the needed oxygen to stay alive. *Poor Kitty!*

My nursing training kicks in, and I immediately assess the need to free her head, or she'll die from suffocation and dehydration alone in this cold tundra.

"I'll hold her body, and you try wiggling the jar off," I say to Mary with my confident nursing voice. Even as I tell myself, *Stay calm! Do not let the cat go, or you won't be able to catch it again.*

Inserting IVs and bedside manners aren't the most critical nursing skills. Emergency medical management, especially staying composed, is a vital nursing skill continually being tested today in the village.

My first nursing instructor asked me, "What is the most dangerous chemical for a patient experiencing a medical emergency?"

I guessed the illegal drug fentanyl, as there are hundreds of deaths a year from this drug in Anchorage. I thought I was being clever to think outside the typical hospital pharmaceuticals by guessing an illegal street drug.

She shook her head. *No.*

I guessed again. "Is it the lifesaving drug that I fail to give them?"

This clever answer was incorrect, too. The nursing professor explains how the most dangerous chemical in an emergency is "Your own adrenaline. Adrenaline makes a nurse forget basic assessment and lifesaving skills."

She then taught us to take deep breaths, focus on the ABCs of assessing a patient (Airway, Breathing, and Circulation), and above all else, stay calm to give the needed treatment. Being composed allows us to properly assess and help the patient – creating a calm atmosphere in an emergency.

I remember my lesson and take a deep, cleansing breath, remaining calm. *I will save this cat! I can do it.*

Mary grips the jar, and I hold onto the cat tightly.

"Let's do this. 1-2-3. PULL!" I command.

"Pop!" Miraculously, the cat's matted black head plops out, with the jar's suction broken. She starts meowing and twisting in my hands.

"Darn it!" I say, dropping the scared cat as her claws rip through my jacket and into my arm.

Chapter 10

Elder Mary

"Gary, get out the healing kit," I command my brother as I gently guide Riley into the school while firmly gripping her forearm tightly to stop the bleeding.

Without hesitation, my brother swiftly springs into action. Gary removes herbs drying in the window, places them in a mortar with seal oil, and grinds them to a paste deftly as I assist Riley in sitting in his office.

I gently remove her jacket and long-sleeve shirt, careful not to jostle her injured arm. My heart races, seeing Riley with her t-shirt stretched tautly across her petite frame and round breasts.

Focus, Mary! You are an elder, I remind myself.

"Here," Gary distracts me, handing me the bowl. He scowls, reading my thoughts.

"This is a traditional healing medicine. You start to feel better right away," I explain.

Riley nods, her gaze fixed on her bloody arm. The wound is large and dripping without her thin outerwear covering the injury. Riley closes her eyes at the gruesome arm, turning away as I tend to it.

I apply the fragrant oily mixture to her deep scratches running from her elbow to her wrist. I rub and hold her arm, moving the body's energy, or as she would call it, *circulation*, to hasten the healing properties.

"The bleeding is stopping. And this prevents infection," I clarify.

Gary chimes in, "Our mom is a renowned herbalist. She taught us Yup'ik traditional remedies. I'm Gary, Bob's brother and the informal Portlock principal."

"Nice to meet you, Gary. Thank you for this," Riley responds.

"We don't usually treat outsiders with our traditional medicines. You can trust that I've used this on myself, my family, and my students without any infections resulting from injuries. I can tell you more about its origins if you want?" Gary volunteers. This is generous of him, as he opposes outsiders and avoids them.

In that regard, we are on opposite sides of the spectrum. I believe sharing our culture will increase understanding and benefit our People. Gary believes outsiders will only use the information to harm our people.

I am happy to see Gary accepting Nurse Riley and talking openly with her. Is his change of heart related to villagers returning from the post office and telling him positive things about Nurse Riley? Or, more than likely, a shared hatred for Trevor and her upcoming student visit is softening his heart to our new nurse.

While Riley talks about herbs with Gary, I reassess this outsider, the city nurse. Riley stunned me by spotting the distressed cat in the dark tundra. Her swift response saved the cat but resulted in her own wounds, which she neither complains about nor blames on the feral cat.

Logically, this traditional remedy will cure her within a few days, as the recipe has healed people for centuries. So there's no need for my heart to race with concern for her. The herbs will stop Riley's infection from spreading and prevent her from needing an emergency hospital evacuation.

My heart defies my logic and continues hammering against my chest.

Returning to the conversation, I attempt to rein in my emotions.

"Being the principal and administering first aid, you're an important elder to know in Portlock," Riley remarks. "And thank you, again, for rescuing my injured arm. My bad luck seems to be following me throughout my visit here."

"No problem. Ptarmigan willow, moss, and seal oil are always handy in a pinch. Especially in a school, children walk in with scrapes and bruises all day," Gary says. "Bob would've applied this same balm if you were closer to his cabin."

I smile in agreement, kicking myself for not detouring and taking her to my cabin to treat her arm. Right now, I could be tending to her, alone in my cabin, and learning more about her without the village watching us.

Gary adds, "As far as your bad luck goes, it sounds like it started on the plane ride over."

She nods and purses her lips, muttering, "Trevor."

"Gary is also not a fan of his." I leave out the part of him not liking *any outsiders.* "As a village elder, he runs the school unofficially," I inform Riley, changing the subject.

"Why not officially?" She asks.

I glance at Gary, allowing him to answer the loaded question, and ready myself for his usual tirade against the government, outsiders, and systematic white oppression.

"I didn't obtain the outside schooling and credentials the government requires. While Bob went to the city's university for his flight training and certifications, I've never left our village." He explains, thankfully a tamer explanation than I expected him to tell her.

He shrugs adding, "The government thinks you must have a degree to prove you can teach our children. But every year, the government sends us a new principal, and he quits within a few weeks of teaching in our mixed, one-room classroom."

"Then Gary takes over and does an amazing job, incorporating our traditions with the textbook's teaching," I interject, proud of my brother's accomplishments in teaching our children. I want Riley to understand the village issues and my brother's contributions which the government doesn't recognize or pay him to do. He is the most important elder in our village, by my estimation.

"Thus, I'm the official school secretary and unofficial principal. I organize and manage the school and kids' education. Our community values our children, and it's an honor to help guide them," Gary says.

Shaking my head at the stupid government's insistence on degrees and teaching plans for our village school, I admire Gary's gift and passion. His teaching credentials are evident in the successful graduation of our students. They even pass the government's minimal core standards tests allowing them their high school diplomas.

Gary stayed in the village. He found work at the school, organizing village meetings and assisting with teaching while becoming a respected elder for our People. I want to convince Gary to leave the village and experience Anchorage to grow his understanding of the outside world.

While I acquired flight experience, my university education, and meeting outsiders, allowed me to let go of my biases against white people. We both became elders but by very different routes. I became an elder by understanding and accepting the outside world, like leveraging government processes and being part of larger tribal organizations to get our village money and support.

"Gary also handles scheduling, managing, and organizing in Portlock and the surrounding villages from this desk," I gesture toward his cluttered workspace with calendars, CB radios, flight schedules, village directories, and open directories of neighboring villages.

The scattered directories and messy desk mean my brother has been calling to locate Trevor and Riley's missing vaccines.

"Any news on the flu vaccine supplies?" Riley asks, reading my mind and stops fussing with her arm injury.

I read Gary's frown as Riley skips the necessary village small talk and moves into discussing her work.

He gruffly responds, "I'll locate them. Let's focus on you meeting the students and eating a bowl of Rena's delicious salmon chowder."

Her face relaxes in relief, and she doesn't recognize her offense to Gary. She seems calmer and trusts Gary to plan her school visit and find the vaccines, which shows her respect for him.

The wind howls as Gary discusses the students with Riley, and she asks questions about their traditional curriculum, which is intertwined with the Alaska state-required education.

I look out the window at the arctic gusts, continuing to escalate without subsiding. The school will become Riley's sanctuary for the night if a snowstorm hits, as planes will be grounded. The school serves as our emergency shelter and makeshift hotel when needed. We lay mats on the cafeteria/gym floor - since there are no hotels or Airbnbs in the village.

However, if the weather changes, snowing Riley in, I will offer her my cabin to stay over in.

My heart starts quickening, thinking about spending time alone with her. I imagine us staying in my cozy wood-fired cabin with the one fur-lined bed and looking outside. I hope for snow.

Chapter 11

Nurse Riley

"Bob, everything is under control," Gary says. Turning to me, he asks, "Riley, are you ready for the school tour?"

Despite the initial fear of infection from the cat scratching down my arm, the traditional balm and careful wrapping work wonders. The pain is subsiding, and the bandages show no sign of bleeding. Learning about Inuit healing practices and cultural education is actually quite enjoyable.

More importantly, I'm relieved I can continue my village adventure, especially with the principal taking charge of finding my vaccines. I'm excited to tour the school, see the clinic, and meet Portlock's youngest villagers.

"Why not!" I respond, smiling. The school is warm and welcoming. Plus, I had to visit the school per my agenda, as it houses the village clinic, and the village elders meet here. I can still complete some of my original trip goals, even if I must cancel my flu clinic.

"The clinic is in the back, and you'll see an exam table with random supplies. I plan on your flu clinic being done in the school commons," Gary explains.

"Sounds great," I reply. His confidence in finding my vaccines and his continued preparations for the flu clinic make me more confident everything will work out.

"Fucking Trevor," I hear Mary mutter under her breath.

She regarded her brother quietly and let him explain the schooling and herbs to me. Contrasting city introductions, where people often welcome each other enthusiastically and talk over each other.

At the post office, I noticed Mary gives others respectful nods and asks pointed questions about their family after greeting them. She knows everything happening in the village, from Max's new video gaming controller to Margo's blue flower beading project.

I noted her quiet interaction in my nursing village notes. When I return to the Anchorage nursing office, I'll research the Yup'ik subtle communication style. *Do Yup'ik people talk less than white people?* A quiet culture explains the villagers' curt conversations with me.

"Trevor," Gary frowns as we walk from the clinic area through the school. "I hear he was showing off and almost crashed. Sorry about that. The flight into Portlock is usually peaceful and awe-inspiring. Sometimes,

I try to imagine what our ancestors think, seeing their children flying above the village like crows."

The radio crackles and Gary returns to the desk to check the CB.

Mary points. "Here are the classrooms. We built four but only use two and the other two are used for Sunday morning service and council meetings." Mary points into a darkened classroom with chairs lined up, a back table with a coffee station, and Bibles stacked in the back.

"Do you employ a priest?" I didn't realize Portlock did church services and had no notes on the religious services here.

"The Catholic church sends summer missionaries, and in the winter, we meet, pray, and drink coffee together," she answers.

Gary appears with a smile. "We found Trevor."

Great! I exhale my tension, and Mary slaps Gary's shoulder.

"Dolores, from up the river, found your bags in their mail. She'll bring it down the river to us," he adds.

Relief floods me. "Thank you," I hug Gary in gratitude. I'm not a hugger, but he saved me thousands of dollars in lost medical supplies and probably my nursing job. I can do the flu clinic, and I haven't failed at my first village trip.

Mary chuffs him again. "Dolores, huh? Wasn't she here a few days ago, dropping another package at school?"

Gary pauses and clenches his jaw. "She's helpful- and if you'd thoroughly checked the plane, she wouldn't need to deliver it," Gary shoots back.

If I had to guess, I'd say that Dolores is Gary's close friend, and Mary is ribbing him. Portlock is a small village – I imagine dating here is difficult when half the town is your relation.

I wonder if Mary is in a relationship. How can I ask her or Gray without my question seeming unprofessional or inappropriate?

Before I formulate the question, Mary asks him, "Does that mean I'm hosting dinner?"

"Gary can't cook," she explains to me.

He laughs, "No. You're hosting a *party*. Break out the pizzas – I put the word out. The nurse's welcome party is at your cabin after school."

He turns to me, "The vaccines won't be here for two hours. It'll be a great way to socialize with the villagers and learn about our community."

"Strange how this sounds like you organized it *before* the vaccines went missing. You have been trying to eat my pizzas all week," Mary remarks.

He punches her on the shoulder, and they both grin, looking more like siblings than village elders.

Thank God! I'm happy to socialize with the vaccines found. It will also allow me to recruit villagers to get their flu shots. I want to hit my goals.

"You did ask for my help, and the party is payment for helping you—"

Before he finishes, an excited teenager appears, latching on to my unharmed arm.

"Lunchtime! Mr. Gary promises we are meeting you during our lunch hour," she says, leading me to an open area with tables set up.

"That is Stacy, our future village nurse," Gary calls out.

"Nice to meet you," I say to her.

She leads me to sit at the table filled with teenagers and places a bowl of salmon chowder before me. Less than thirty students are seated around the different tables, sorted more or less by age. And they are laughing over their chowder while watching me. The students are the loudest villagers I've met here.

"Stacy, you only get her for lunch hour. She needs to get ready," Mary calls over to us.

"We heard - Pizza?"

She nods, and Stacy whispers, "Bob hides Pizza Hut in his freezer."

Pizza Hut? Apparently, the junk food attraction works on village teenagers, too.

"I'm excited to meet a future nurse. I graduated from the University of Anchorage's Nursing Program just recently. Go ahead and ask me whatever you want to know," I tell Stacy.

"Is anyone else thinking about going to university?" I ask the teen table.

Unsurprisingly, only a few kids raised their hands. Most villagers stay in their home villages and continue fishing on their family's boats because it's safe. Choosing city education is a big deal, and I plan to encourage these kids, especially Stacy. Portlock needs medical resources, and having a local villager as their nurse is the perfect solution.

"I'm Ellen, and I'll be going to business school. I'm already selling my furs, but I want to get the accounting stuff," a confident teen with braids explains.

"She's already a successful seamstress and furrier," Stacy explains.

I ask Stacy, "Do you want to help me organize the flu clinic later?"

Before she responds, I overhear Gary asking Mary, "The nurse is rather attractive for a cheechako, don't you think?"

Before I hear the answer, the teens barrage me with questions about Anchorage and how they can help me at the pizza party later.

I strain to hear Mary's answer over their voices.

Stacy asks, "Do you get your own room at university? I share mine with my brothers right now . . ."

Amidst the teens' lively conversation, I hear pieces of Mary's response, ". . . very city-white. . .my type. . . tonight."

The kids' excitement drowns out her voice as the younger students crowd around to ask me questions as they meet me.

Chapter 12

Elder Mary

"Are you next, Mary?"

I smile at Riley, waving for me to join the students' noisy lunch table, presently converted into a makeshift hairdressing station.

The students' compliments of her twisted hair morphed into a pop-up hair salon. And hair bands and a brush materialize as she styles the student's hair while discussing the university and city life with them.

I don't want to disrespect the nurse, but fussing over my hair isn't my thing. The school kids turn to me, judging and adding pressure to my response to the new nurse.

"Of course," I say, sitting on the floor since I tower over her petite frame with my five-foot-ten height.

In the village school, I towered over the boys, and although my family's statuesque height makes me proud, I wish I wasn't the tallest girl growing up in our small school. It was another glaring difference which set me apart.

Riley brushes through my hair with her fingertips, then pulls back and parts my thick mane. Her fingers dance lightly over my forehead and scalp. She removes a few strands to land softly around my face and runs her fingers slowly through the back.

"Your hair is beautiful," she whispers.

Her breath warms my neck, igniting a passionate fluttering in my chest.

"Thank you," I respond.

Somehow she answers the student's unending questions about city life: where she eats, what her Starbucks coffee order is, what American Eagle's mall window is displaying, and she pivots, describing starting university in Anchorage. She shares her struggles to fit in, learning to study for her classes, and suddenly becoming qualified to care for patients as a nurse.

The students laugh when she tells them about buying a nightgown she mistook for an elegant dress. They hang onto her every word as she talks about her university time, a roommate who didn't flush the toilet, how she attempted to start an IV upside down, and when she accidentally took a final exam in the wrong class.

Riley's openness is what the sheltered village kids need to hear to relate to outsiders and maybe someday leave our village. She senses their unasked questions and worries about the unfamiliar, bigger world outside of Portlock. She answers their silly questions by telling them how she overcame her fears. Her empathy for the village youth makes me smile inside. She is not the average outsider. She listens and cares about their future and their day-to-day life.

The students react to her enthusiasm in meeting them and ask more questions about the city as she braids and brushes through their hair. Even the boys are sporting Riley's braids and buns, to their delight and Gary's horror.

She explains to the boys, "You can keep your hair long in the city, too. Stylish city guys let their hair cascade to their shoulders or sport a man bun for work."

Her hands glide through my straight, black hair. Her fingers are hot and light, giving me chills. I smell her lavender soap, and her lithe body touching and resting against my back gives me chills. With her soft body against mine, she reaches for a hair tie on the table. She leans back into me, weaving the elastic band around her delicate wrist as she tightens the braid.

An intense chemistry storm explodes inside of me, approximating the science class reaction Gary does when he pours baking soda into vinegar. My toes, to the ends of my hair, fizzle from her touch. I am grounded to Riley's warm hands and floating on the high from her contact.

"To class, all of you," Gary yells across the cafeteria, stopping the city hairstyles before it moves to his braidable beard.

The students snap to attention at Gary's voice, rushing back to the classroom, dropping their bowls in the sink, and calling out, "See you later," mainly to Riley.

My brother cocks his head and raises his brows at the odd sight of me getting my hair braided by her. He frowns and gives me a stern older brother glare, transmitting the message, *She's a dangerous outsider,* and, *Do not trust her.*

I usually tie my raven hair back and forget about it. I am not a girly, touchy person, nor do I befriend outsiders, but Riley is different.

I'm thankful Gary called the students to class. Now, I can enjoy Riley's hands skimming my scalp to braid my hair without an audience. I recognize my longing for her touch and my femininity bubbling inside me, responding to her infectious joy.

She fills the silence by humming Lady Gaga's "Born This Way." Her refusal to appreciate the blissful quiet is becoming more endearing than annoying.

I find myself humming along to her gentle voice. Usually, meaningless noise bothers me, but not Riley's.

"The kids are awesome," she says. "Also, the chowder is the best cafeteria food I've ever eaten."

"We enjoy the best cook, kitchen and ingredients," I say. "Rena cooks us local foods, using Yup'ik recipes."

"Rena is the food pantry manager from the Post Office, right?" Riley asks.

"Yes." I am sure she saw the hair situation and decided to leave without greeting the nurse again.

Riley continues, "Stacy's quite clever. I'm glad she's considering nursing school. UAA has an excellent medical school, too. Would she consider becoming a doctor? Or is that too much?"

I'm pleasantly surprised Riley asks me my opinion on Stacy's schooling. Riley is not the same as other outsiders - she is trying to respect our culture and understand the villagers.

"Stacy is scientifically-minded and smart. Being a nurse is a big dream - and leaving the village for city education. Telling her she could be a doctor is comparable to telling her she could be a time traveler. Living in a city and becoming a nurse is a big stretch for her," I explain.

"She's met the grade requirements and is motivated. Should I not mention it then?" Riley persists.

"No. You can tell her. Sometimes Gary and I forget village children dream big, like the city kids do. Dreaming isn't exclusive to the city. We don't push their imaginations far enough," I say, oversharing in my relaxed state.

"Okay," She responds. With her hand lingering on my hair, she ties my braid and sets the end on my shoulder.

"You've inspired them and made the city less scary. I'm glad you came here," I tell her as her clear eyes meet mine, making my heart dance. I place my hand over her soft, small hand.

She meets my eyes, unblinking, and her cheeks redden.

"Let's head to my place. We need to organize a party," I interrupt the moment to stand, moving a respectful step away.

"What?" She scrunches her nose cutely.

"Gary will call us when your vaccines arrive. There's time," I explain.

I move further away before the moment becomes a tangible, memorable connection. I'm not ready to give my heart away to an outsider.

Grabbing our bowls, I drop them into the sink and holler a *thank you* to Rena, who is hiding in the back, scrubbing the kitchen—no doubt still avoiding the city nurse and her hairstyling. Rena's raven, silver hair sweeps down to her waist.

I grab an extra parka from the hook by the door. Riley needs to wear a warmer jacket for the ride to my cabin. Then, I tell myself, *I'd wrap any outsider in a fur parka. I want to keep Riley warm because I am a concerned village elder, keeping everyone safe, not because I care for her.*

Of course, I'd prefer to keep Riley warm and safe by wrapping her tight and cozy in my arms tonight. I look out the window, and there's no snow or clouds.

Riley shakes me from my steamy thoughts, asking *the question.*

"Why do people call you *Bob*?"

Chapter 13

Nurse Riley

Mary stands before me, and my fingers tingle from her soft hair as her firm hand covers mine. My heart flutters in an unfamiliar way. She's a stunning, powerful Alaskan woman.

No! My morning is disastrous enough. I cannot be distracted by my attraction to Mary. Not because she's a woman or a Yup'ik Elder, but because my plan doesn't include falling in love. *I don't have time.*

And *not today*, on the first day of my first nursing job in a village far from home. I shake my head and sigh.

Falling in love can happen *after* becoming the Alaska Community Health Director in ten years. My energy and passion are for my nursing career, not dating. I'm providing care to villages lacking access to medical care. I'm making a difference by giving culturally- appropriate interventions that respect traditions and the villagers' health and wellness.

Chasing love and dating is not a priority—*I must stay focused!*

I move my hand from hers and redirect her by asking her the question I'm waiting to ask. "Mary, why do the villagers call you Bob?"

Mary moves to the door and freezes, her hand on a parka. I wonder if I've accidentally offended her with my question. I only asked as a distraction to our intimate moment and didn't expect her nickname to be a big deal.

The mood gets heavy, and her shoulders tighten.

I open my mouth, ready to apologize, but she begins talking.

"When I started school, the teacher told us to introduce ourselves with our preferred name. I introduced myself as *Bob* because I didn't really identify with being *Mary* or even a girl. I enjoyed fishing and hunting, so it felt more natural. Bob fits me better than Mary."

She looked at me and tilted her head to see if I wanted to hear more. I nod.

"I have always been into the outdoors, mechanics, and working with my hands. I am a confident person, and I'm unafraid to stand up and speak for our village, which is more of a masculine role in the traditional culture. Although as I get older, I am discovering that I enjoy my feminine aspects too. I appreciate my long hair, beading, and working with my mother to collect herbs, which are seen as more traditional female roles."

I remain silent and lean closer to her, asking, "So you don't feel fully female or masculine?"

She shrugs and says, "It's more I don't want to be labeled with either, and I acknowledge that I'm more than one thing - I have many talents. I'm *me*. Growing up in Portlock, villagers accept me without forcing me to confine myself to a gender or pronoun. Yup'ik call this two-spirited, and our people celebrate it as a special quality," she says.

"Oh, I didn't know. I hope I didn't overstep by asking," I say, biting my bottom lip with an apology ready. She smiles and continues before I can apologize.

"Everyone is curious, but most are afraid to ask. I'm honored to share my story and more about myself with you," she reassures me, handing me the fur parka. "I'm a respected elder, a pilot, a family member, and a friend. Those roles are not gendered. Villagers don't label and separate each other. We accept our community for who we are and for our abilities."

I nod, and I'm happy she felt comfortable to share with me.

"I haven't talked about being two-spirited in a long time."

"Well, you embody the strength of both energies," I add. I smile at her explanation and reflect on the differences I experienced growing up and even as an adult, wishing everyone was as accepting as the villagers.

"Yes, as a two-spirited person, I nurture and don't hide my energy, whether people would call it masculine or feminine energy. I am in touch with my strength and my caring," she explains.

"I do understand about not fitting in," I say with a shrug. "Thank you for taking the time to explain it to me and trusting me with your truth. I've heard the term two-spirited, but I didn't fully understand it." Now I understand Mary's strength and uniqueness that I sensed when I met her. I hold the warm, fur-lined parka she handed me closely.

"Living and fitting in here is easier than the city. Sometimes it's easier to ignore the ignorance rather than educate every person I meet. When I'm in the city, people see me as a Inuit woman and call me *Mary*. My family calls me *Bob*," she says.

"What would you like me to call you?" I ask, hoping she chooses the villager's term and not the outsider's name for her.

"Mary is perfect. I like Bob, but when I'm with you, the feminine energy feels stronger and I think I fit the name Mary, better," she says, fingering the braid.

I'm a little disappointed that she doesn't want me to call her Bob, but knowing that she's thought about it and chose *Mary* because of our shared feminine energy makes sense. She's right that I was trying to place a role, a gender, and my ideas on her because of my expectations and norms. She's perfect, and I'll respect her by using whatever name she wants.

"Mary, you better watch out, or I'll pull out my makeup kit next and see how much female energy I can ignite in you," I joke, pulling out my lipstick.

"No!" she adds, "I'm not changing, but you have the most girly-feminine spirit I've seen." She shakes her head, "I didn't say that right. I mean, *you are* a *breath-taking, unique woman* with or without makeup. I'm happy you're here."

A rosy blush creeps into my cheeks, and I'm grateful for applying extra makeup to help mask how her compliment embarrasses me.

"Riley, I draw the line at makeup. I do like the braid, though. Come on, let's head out. After all, my brother worked hard to organize Dolore's visit, and I'm eager to eat my Pizza Hut stash," Mary says.

"Shouldn't I wait here for the vaccines?" I ask.

"We have time. It takes an hour to travel here from the next village," she explains.

"What's the big deal with Pizza Hut, anyway?" I ask.

"There are no pizza restaurants around here, so I bring in special foods from Anchorage and surprise people with them," she says.

"Awesome idea," I say.

She leans in, telling me, "I'm not popular for being an elder. My fast food stash is the secret." She winks.

I'm sure it's more than her pizza stash, which makes her well-loved. Mary is thoughtful, resourceful, and beautiful, drawing me to her.

"You'll see. Next time you visit, bring a box of Taco Bell supreme burritos. The whole village will come and greet you on the airfield." She laughs.

"Thanks for the tip. And for your help. I couldn't have done this without you," I thank her, not wanting her to move away from me.

She pulls on her parka and pauses, taking it off, handing it to me, and taking the one she placed in my arms earlier.

"Here. Wear my warmer parka. I lined it in the spotted seal from last year's hunt. Plus, the red and blue enhance your glowing skin and blue eyes," she says.

She noticed my blue eyes and embarrassing red cheeks. Maybe she's interested in me, too? I shake my head. Or she's simply observant.

It is probably just a village custom to bestow a parka to visitors.

I switched parkas and noticed the weight and warmth of her parka. "This is amazing," I say while gently running my fingers along the soft fur and carefully tracing the beaded pattern with my fingertips.

"My grandmother taught me to bead and you already met our local furrier, Ellen, who sewed the lining in that."

The parka is beautiful; I assumed it was a family heirloom. I'm surprised the intricate beading came from Mary's hands. She surprises me, and I feel special regardless of her casual intent. I'm honored, and I remember the lesson she taught me at the airport about graciously accepting gifts.

"Thank you. I'm honored to accept and wear your parka," I tell her from under my lashes and blush.

Before she responds, Gary appears with a frown, surveying me wearing Mary's parka and her braided hair. "The kids are using your truck for a diesel engine lesson. Can you take the quad?"

"Sure," she responds, stepping further away from me.

A quad? I have no clue what they're talking about.

Chapter 14

Nurse Riley

The braid over Mary's shoulder highlights her femininity, and I can't stop staring. Her brown eyes catch the light, and the golden flecks sparkle, stealing my attention. I forget why I'm here, in Portlock, standing in the school. My question and my worries vanish.

She smiles, "Are you ready for a ride?"

As I zip up the parka, I discover two hidden treasures in its pockets, a snug hat and mittens. They promise me warmth and comfort on the ride. The chilly weather calls for protection, and the small gesture of providing these to me, assures me Mary cares about my well-being.

Whatever this unknown ride is to wherever Mary lives, I'll need to stay warm in the chilly weather, and I trust she will explain what is going on.

"Okay," I say, my anticipation building.

"I'll call when Dolores arrives with the vaccines," Gary interjects, his voice carrying from behind us as we step into the cold air.

These two elders run the town and have the necessary village knowledge. I trust their judgment.

If they're confident in my vaccines getting here for me to do my clinic, I'm sure I can trust their judgment.

"Did you enjoy the school tour?" Mary asks, leading me to the small school garage.

"I did, but I must say, I am still thinking about Rena's delicious chowder," I respond. I'm not being polite, either - Rena's deliciously thick, creamy chowder filled with fresh salmon, potato, onion, and celery chunks. I've eaten chowder at expensive restaurants, but this authentic chowder is so much better.

Mary swings open the large outer garage door, revealing a formidable sight — an immense 4-wheeled vehicle, open to the elements without a roof or doors.

The quad resembles a kid's monster truck toy with oversized tires - definitely not a safe, cozy ride.

Oh God, how will I drive this? There's no steering wheel, gas, or brake pedal!

"This is our ride." Mary must be reading my thoughts because she adds, stepping closer to the 4-wheeler, "I'll drive the quad. My cabin is close by."

Thank goodness! She's driving. Despite being born and raised in Alaska, I can barely manage a 4-wheeler, especially one that requires shifting gears. *Maybe I am a Cheechako outsider.* Luckily, I do not have to admit my ignorance.

Gracefully, Mary mounts the 4-wheeler, inserting the key as the vehicle rumbles to life, and she gestures for me to join her.

I cautiously throw my leg over the back settling in behind her, mindful of maintaining a professional distance. *I am a nurse committed to professionalism even in these unexpected circumstances, like being close enough to hug Mary's warm body.*

"What do I need to do to ride on this?" I inquire, peeking a sideways glance at her. I am clueless even about riding the quad. I refuse to further embarrass myself in front of the villagers by making a silly mistake riding the quad. They already label me as a *Cheechako.*

Mary guides my hands from the seat, instructing me to wrap my arms around her waist which creates an unprofessional blush across my cheeks.

"Hold on tight," she advises.

In an instant, we are off, tires spewing rocks and snow as they spin against the hard-packed Alaskan village road. As we ride out into the wind, I instinctively press my body closer against Mary's.

The quad travels smoothly over bumps, like a caribou navigating the backcountry easily. I bet these tires wouldn't get stuck even with deep snow or muddy roads. *No wonder they use 4-wheelers in the villages; the beasts are fantastic at galloping across the tundra.*

Despite the chilly wind, I am cozy and warm nestled against Mary in her furry parka.

The trees blur past us, and we seem to be the only people on the road. The speeding rush of wind and freedom are exhilarating. We veer off the dirt road, passing through a clump of trees, and arrive at a forested cabin beside a tranquil lake.

I take in the crisp air and the idyllic surroundings. Mary's picturesque cabin is enchanting. How did she find such a serene spot, nestled by a crystal blue lake, engulfed by trees covered in icy glitter?

She brings the 4-wheeler to a halt by the front door, and as I unclasp my arms from her waist, inadvertently tumbling backward off the quad.

I sprawl on the cold, hard ground, gazing at the clouds above me. The chill seeps into my body, and I quickly assess myself — no sharp pain, blood, broken bones, and a clear head. My nursing brain tells me I'm alright - no concussion or severe injury. I've bruised my pride, and only a Cheechako dismounts a quad by falling backward into the gravel.

"Are you okay?" Mary rushes to my side, concern etched across her face. Her worried eyes provide me with temporary comfort. I wish I sustained a severe injury or got knocked out.

Amid Mary's worried expression, unexpected laughter escapes my lips. No matter how hard I strive to maintain professionalism, fate conspires to put me on my backside. *Quite literally*, this time.

I'm *the worst* at being a professional! This is my first day as their village nurse. *OMG, I must stop laughing!* The thought causes the opposite effect, making me giggle even more uncontrollably.

Mary shakes her head, trying not to laugh but can't contain it. Before long, she is laughing with me. Her deep, loud laugh transforms her serious face into a young girl's—her worries released, and she abandons her respectful elder demeanor as she reaches out to help me up.

I impulsively grab her arm and playfully pull her down to the icy ground with me. Between giggles, I tell her, "I'm only dying of embarrassment, Mary. My pride is hurt, but I'll survive!"

"Not a bad view down here," she says, looking up at me.

Is she talking about the cloudy sky or me?

Rather than posing the question, I respond, giggling, "Your cabin is incredible. It's a picturesque Alaskan wilderness postcard."

"Come on," Mary says, rising to her feet and turning to help me up. "The inside is even cozier, with a roaring fire and steaming hot chocolate waiting for us."

Mary's strength is evident as she lifts my stiff, cold body and half-carries me into her cabin. She settles me by the wood stove's smoldering fire, and she's right. I notice the cozy ambiance—rustic furniture, plush furs adorning the chairs, and the crackling flames' warmth. The experience is better than a postcard!

"Hot chocolate?" she offers.

"Absolutely," I reply eagerly, attempting to mask the fluttering in my chest. "But will you promise not to tell anyone about my Cheechako 4-wheeler dismount?"

I worry my fall will erase the confidence I projected while meeting the teenagers at the school and villagers at the Post Office.

"You are a *real* Alaskan woman, and I only saw you being that." Mary responds, starting her kettle.

I regard her with gratitude. The serene cabin reflects Mary perfectly—*awe-inspiring*. Mary goes above and beyond, from guiding my plane to safety, enabling me to embrace the village experience, tending to my injured arm, and now rescuing me from my embarrassing fall. I came here to assist the village, but she's helping me understand her village culture through her kindness.

Chapter 15

Elder Mary

The rich hot chocolate aroma permeates the air as I stir in a dash of cinnamon with the milk in a hefty, slightly-misshapen clay mug. This mug is a special gift from the student's traditional pottery class, representing our tribe's past and future. I am lost in my thoughts of clay and art when Riley's voice breaks through.

"Mary, thank you again," she says, waking me from thoughts of digging up more clay for the art class next week. She's staring at me from under a pile of furs in front of the wood stove.

I pause momentarily, unsure what she's thanking me for – *the rescue, the hot chocolate, or the fire's warmth.* Smiling, I respond, "All part of the welcoming service." And I hand her the steaming mug.

She uses both hands to cradle it, and there's no jewelry on her pale fingers to indicate a partner in Anchorage. She blows and takes a sip ending with a satisfying moan, making me laugh again. Clearly, she enjoys hot chocolate.

I add this to my mental list: *Riley loves hot chocolate.* Strangely, I find myself drawn to her, subconsciously cataloging her *likes* and paying attention to the details, despite her being an outsider.

Riley, a young white, government nurse from the city, represents the force changing our village's future. While I, as an esteemed Yup'ik elder, hold the responsibility of managing the community and representing our tribe in Anchorage. I lead and advocate for our people and our traditions, safeguarding our history, while Riley influences the government health funds for our village.

I shake my head, thinking of her falling off the quad. *I said I'd forget, and I will. Anyone could fall off a s4-wheeler, not just a city girl.*

"Village nursing must be different than working in the city," I say, hoping to encourage her to share more details about herself and her personal life.

"Yes—"

The door crashes open before Riley finishes her response, and Stacy, accompanied by her friend Max, stumbles in, laughter filling the room as they stomp the dirt and ice off their boots.

"Gary sent us to help you set up and tell you that Dolores is on her way with the medical supplies. She'll be here in less than an hour," Stacy announces with a broad smile.

I bet Gary sent them to ensure I had no alone time to bond with the outsider. I won't let my brother thwart my plan to get to know Riley better.

"Can I drink some hot chocolate?" Max asks, wandering into the kitchen.

"There's no time for that," I say. I will make this party and Riley's visit successful because she deserves it. Helping the nurse might start a new relationship between our village and the Alaska Community Health Department.

"Max, you are on food duty—reheat the pizzas, and cut up the vegetables," I direct while going to the kitchen. I pull the pizzas from my chest freezer and put carrots and celery on the cutting board. I turn the oven on to preheat.

Max begins pouring himself a hot chocolate and starts walking to the couch.

"Max!" I say, intercepting him and handing him a notepad. "Write this down: six pizzas, cook at 425 degrees. Two at a time for twenty minutes. Then clear the counters and set out plates, napkins, and silverware. You know your aunties will bring food."

I am in full planning mode. If I can't be alone with Riley, I'll make her party a smashing success so the village loves the new nurse, and Riley will love our little community and return.

Max scribbles furiously, but I know the village women will take over the kitchen once they arrive. In our village, hosting potlucks means everyone pitches in, and my home becomes a comfortable gathering place for the community.

Turning to Riley, I announce, "Your flu clinic will be done here, alongside the potluck."

I raise my hand to stall any of her objections. "My bedroom is spacious and private. You can give flu shots privately there and then join in the festivities out here."

"Wait... here?" Riley responds, shaking her head in surprise.

"I promise it will be better than the school clinic's clunky storage room, and everyone will be here tonight. Trust me," I assure her, leading her and Stacy to my bedroom, grateful that I keep my home tidy.

"Start making a list of what you'll need, and Stacy will assist you in setting up."

Riley gazes around my bedroom, her eyes lingering on the sizable wooden-framed bed adorned with furs. She nods, picking up a pen and notepad from my desk.

"Okay. I trust you." Riley says, tapping her pink lip as she contemplates the logistics.

Stacy asks, "How many chairs do you want in here?"

"Two and another small table," Riley answers firmly. She opens her bag and spreads her papers across my desk.

I step aside as Stacy drags in two extra dining room chairs and places Riley's hot chocolate on the desk. With grace, Riley settles herself at my desk, and seeing her cozily situated in my room takes my breath away.

I force myself to breathe, composing myself. "Stacy, I'm going to fetch more chairs. Tell me, using the radio, if there's anything else I need to grab from the school."

"I'm on it!" she says, flipping her braid over her shoulder, thrilled to be party planning and working with the new nurse.

"Please grab this from the clinic while you are at the school," Riley's hand brushes mine as she hands me her scribbled list.

Riley's list finds a place in my pocket as I walk out into the crisp afternoon, happy to have her in my room, even if it is sharing her with the teenagers. I hide my smile by reading her scribbled list, a bottle of rubbing alcohol, cotton balls, and clipboards.

"Riley is nice, and you guys are a cute couple. I feel the vibe between the two of you," Stacy whispers, joining me in a hushed conversation.

I shake my head and put my finger to my lips. I don't want Riley to overhear this teenage gossip.

"But you could visit her in Anchorage, right? Aren't you going back there next week anyway?" she prods.

I viciously pull my hat on and give her my best, respect-your-elders stare to end the conversation. "She's not Yup'ik," I say simply.

"She's single. I asked her," Max says, joining in and ignoring my stare.

"My relationship status and hers is none of your business. Now focus on setting up for the party you two," I say, herding them back to the kitchen.

"When's the last time you dated?" Stacy continues her inappropriate conversation.

"Many salmon in the stream," I say, a village joke referencing the city saying there are plenty of fish in the sea.

"Winters are long and cold," Stacy adds, returning to help Riley organize as Max nods at me.

Winter in Portlock is endless when there's no one to warm your bed—that's the proverb she refers to, but I don't correct her. The kids mean well, but they are overstepping.

However, they aren't wrong about Riley and my connection. And I haven't dated in a very long time.

Knowing Riley is in my bedroom and will be there all evening makes my heart pump faster, causing me to glance at her, arranging chairs with Stacy.

If Stacy and Max see my attraction to her, I better steer clear of Riley, or the other Elders might notice. A relationship with an outsider does not benefit our traditions or village. I will stay busy and avoid my bedroom tonight.

"I am heading out. Remember to call me if you are missing anything!" I call out, placing her list in my pocket and walking out into the crisp afternoon.

Chapter 16

Nurse Riley

"Are you nervous about the flu clinic?" Stacy's voice jolts me from my trance, my eyes fixed on the door Mary exited.

I trust Mary, but running an immunization clinic out of a house is odd. *Everything about village nursing is unconventional!* At least Mary's cabin is more comfortable and inviting than the school storage room labeled "Clinic."

I take a deep breath, trying to steady myself. "A little, I suppose. Doing an immunization clinic in a house is definitely different from what I'm used to. But with your help, we will make it fantastic."

"I'm excited to help. I want to be a caring nurse like you. And I think you're awesome," Stacy says, bouncing on her toes.

A smile tugs at the corners of my lips. Stacy's enthusiasm is catching. "Thank you, Stacy. That means a lot to me."

Max calls out from the kitchen as we stand, contemplating the task ahead. "Hey, can you guys help?"

Stacy and I laugh, realizing we've left Max alone too long. "I'm on it!" Stacy replies.

"We are done setting up the bedroom— err, clinic— until the vaccines arrive anyway. Go save him," I tell her.

We go to the kitchen, where Max attempts to cut carrots with a bread knife. He could use our assistance.

"I think you need a sharper knife, Max," I suggest, chuckling at his ineffective sawing of the vegetables.

Stacy takes out a well-worn ivory and curved metal ulu, the traditional Alaskan cutting tool. She effortlessly takes over the cutting board and vegetables with practiced ease. I watch in awe as she glides the ulu through the carrots, efficiently slicing them into thin pieces.

"Max, watch and learn," she says, playfully sticking her tongue out at him.

With the food preparations in their hands, I return to Mary's bedroom-turned-clinic. I stack my extra paperwork in the corner, moving an intricately beaded flower on a leather satchel to the bedside table. It will be safer there.

I survey the room. I've disinfected it, added patient seating, a place to wash my hands and pull up the vaccines, and a spot to clean the injection sites and apply bandages. The desk area is transformed into a proper clinic table.

"This will do," I say, nodding to myself. I am getting a little nervous. *What if no one wants a flu shot? What if the villagers tell me not to come back?*

I gather my thoughts and sit on the couch, my lukewarm hot chocolate mug in my hand. The bustling sounds from the kitchen and the sight of the students working together ease my nerves. This community appreciates coming together and supporting each other. They are helping me, and I am sure I will be able to give at least a few flu shots tonight.

The cabin door opens, and the remaining village students arrive in a rush, with more cold air bursting in. The noisy boot stomping and greetings fill the home, making it sound like the party is starting.

"Hi, Riley. Need a hand?" Max's younger sister, Mia, asks me.

"I am set up. I think I will help Max and Stacy with the food," I explain.

"Mia, you straighten the boots and move the jackets to Bob's guest room bed," Stacy orders.

The students, well-versed in the tasks, hurriedly shove furniture aside and clear countertops. Piles of flight documents get moved into stacks and tucked safely under cabinets.

I sit on the couch, observing all of them, still sporting the buns and braids from our lunchtime meeting.

Seeing them buzzing about and happy chases away my nerves, and I relax into the comfy furs.

Max plops on the couch beside me, and his excitement is palpable.

I turn to him, curious about his family. "Where's the rest of your family?"

"They're coming. By the time I arrived home from school, everyone already heard about the party. And nobody is missing Pizza Hut! My mom is making a dish to bring, something even a Cheechako will enjoy," Max winks at me.

"Max!" Mia cries. "I told our mom that you are a *REAL* Alaskan, and she's going to bring her famous Eskimo ice cream," she says. "Mom told us we are getting flu shots because she doesn't want sick kids this winter."

"Great!" I'm happy to know I will have two patients. I pray the traditional dish of whale blubber, ground-up fish, sugar, and blueberries will taste better than the description I remember hearing from a classmate in the city who obviously didn't enjoy it.

Max pulls a face and tells Mia, "I never get sick. It's the rest of you."

"Hey, I'm protecting everyone from the flu. I don't want anybody sick and no aunties being rushed to the hospital because they got the flu from *you*," I add as the oven timer dings and the pizza aroma fills the air. "Go, eat some pizza," I tell the kids, shooing the crowd off my comfy couch.

More villagers arrive, and Gary's voice echoes from the radio, "We are on our way with the medical stuff. Over."

Stacy clicks the CB in response and gives me a double thumbs up.

As more and more villagers flock into the cabin, the students welcome them with enthusiastic handshakes, as Max distributes pizza. I watch their camaraderie and let the joyful voices wash over me.

In a frantic motion, Stacy hastily plops beside me and shoves a pizza slice in my hands. I devour it with immense hunger.

"Bob is a pretty awesome person," she starts, her tone lighthearted.

I nod in agreement, chewing on the pizza. "Mary is welcoming and is teaching me alot."

"You guys should date," she proclaims, lifting her eyebrows.

I swallow with my now-dry throat. "I'm your village nurse, and Mary is your village elder. Since we work together, that'd be inappropriate," I stammer my words, my heart pounding in my chest. I wonder if my growing attraction to Mary is glaringly apparent.

Stacy glances at Max, "How do you even know when you should start a relationship?"

She smiles at his antics of rolling the pizza and eating it like a burrito. She adds, "I mean in your professional opinion."

I smile, ready to change the conversation to focus on her. "Healthy relationships start with friendships because that's how you get to know and trust someone. You take a risk and trust that if your friendship works, a relationship will work, too."

Stacy nods, then asks, "Do you already have a partner?"

I shake my head. "No, but I'm too busy *and* I don't want a partner right now," I tell her.

"Healthy relationships start with friendships. You need friends and sometimes you need to take a risk," Stacy echoes with a twinkle in her eyes.

Oh, Snap! Stacy is much more bold and quick-witted than I was at her age!

She adds, "At least consider it. You are both caring people and deserve another good friend."

Before I respond, Gary and Dolores make a grand entrance, striding with pomp and circumstance, weighed down by my precious medical supplies. The villagers whoop and clap as if this is their victory.

Relief washes over me, and I grin. "Thank goodness! The flu clinic is starting."

Stacy waves them into the bedroom to drop their bags, and I unload the vaccines and my supplies to start.

With the clinic ready and supplies in hand, the evening is set for a successful clinic and party. The clinic renews my purpose here, and Stacy starts lining up people for me.

I'm grateful for the support and friends I'm finding in the village.

Chapter 17

Nurse Riley

"Can you leave the information sheet when you've finished reading it?" I asked Meriel since my sheets ran out many patients ago – I'm sharing the last copy to review with the patients.

She returns the sheet to the desk next to my pre-planned clinic schedule.

- *10 am, Set up Clinic at school*
- *11 am, Open Flu Clinic Open – immunize willing students (estimated 5–10 students)*
- *12 pm, Lunch*
- *1 pm, Clean & Restock clinic room*
- *2 pm, Open flu clinic to staff, families, and others (estimated 10–15 adults)*
- *5 pm, Close clinic, Pack Supplies & Clean-up*
- *6 pm, Chart on patient sheets and fill out the required Village Outreach Influenza Immuniza-*

tion Clinic Report

- *7 pm, Airport - Depart to Anchorage*

I glance at the planned schedule on my desk, but it bears little resemblance to the afternoon I've experienced. My intended itinerary for clinical efficiency is replaced with a whirlwind of activity—meeting villagers, socializing, and administering vaccines all evening. Instead of the relaxed fifteen-minute appointments, I rush through each patient interaction, completing the immunization screening questions with seconds to spare before moving on to the next person.

This starkly contrasts with the thorough, systematic approach I learned in nursing school, where we take time to discuss medical histories, address any medical concerns, and gather weights and vital signs. In this fast-paced environment, there's barely enough time for a warm greeting and a quick poke, with many patients waving off the band-aid so the next person can get their vaccine.

Mary surprises me by popping her head in. "I said that you're on break to bring you more food before it's gone. How are you doing?"

Meriel and baby Moe weave around Mary, leaving through the open door she holds—Meriel's Barbie bandaid is showing on her arm, and Moe has one on his chubby thigh.

Mary gracefully spins inside the room with a plate piled high and uses her foot to shut the door firmly behind her.

"You met our youngest villager," she says, setting the plate on the desk.

I ignore my racing heart, tired but excited to have a break and enjoy the quiet of only us in the bedroom. Instead of asking her anything, like if she's seeing anyone, I distract myself by disposing of needles in the plastic sharps container and rubbing on hand sanitizer. I rearrange the medical supplies, straightening them on the desk.

"Moe is adorable. In fact, everyone is great!" I gush, adding, "Stacy is amazing with patient organization, breezing through getting people in and out of the clinic room."

Mary nods, "We are proud of her, and she will be an incredible nurse. Especially with a superb village nurse as her role model."

I blush and hear Stacy outside the door announcing, "The nurse is on a break," followed by disappointed grumblings. *Who would imagine people clamoring to see me?*

I smile, trying to change the subject. "The Barbie band-aids seem to be a hit."

Mary laughs in response. "I overheard Mia explaining that Barbie is actually you. They are Nurse Riley bandaids. We don't have many Barbie dolls here."

Looking at the blonde and pink figure on the bandages makes me laugh. "The program gave me this kit, and these are the only bandages they packed. I'm not sure if it was a first village trip joke or if we really only have Barbie bandaids."

"It's cute either way," she replies.

"I guess I do look a little Barbie-like," I say, fingering my pink jacket.

"Okay, Nurse Barbie. Dig in before we get interrupted," Mary says.

"This smells delicious," I say as I take a fork and sample the different items.

"I made the moose burger."

I hold the burger dripping with bbq sauce, mayonnaise, grilled onions, and cheddar and take a healthy bite which immediately dribbles down my chin.

Mary laughs and swipes my chin with a napkin, as I can't set down the juicy burger without it falling apart.

"Pizza Hut brings them here, and my moose burger makes them stay," she says. "Also, there's no one left for you to immunize. Your clinic is a success."

I set the burger down, wipe my greasy fingers, and review my village flu list. *Mary's right, I vaccinated everyone within record time.*

"A *total* success," I agree. "Portlock may be the first village with a 100% flu vaccination rate."

"The magic of a potlatch and a friendly nurse," she adds with a sly grin.

"No, it's the magic of your community. I'm grateful for you finding my medical supplies, introducing me to everyone, and throwing this incredible gathering. You saved me, and this success is all due to your help. I truly appreciate it." My eyes soften, looking at her gold-flecked eyes as warmth fills me.

Mary meets my gaze, her eyes now intensely black, and places her hand gently on my arm. "No mistaking it, this is *all you.* You made the decision to make it work and embraced our village. The villagers saw how much you cared and your good intentions. They wanted to help you succeed and keep your job to come back here."

A surge of electricity courses through my veins as her hand connects with my arm. Time stands still as we share this charged moment.

"Do you trust me?" Her voice breaks the silence, and her question hangs in the air.

I nod, parting my lips in anticipation.

"Close your eyes and open your mouth," she instructs.

I set down the burger and wipe my hands before I comply, my heart racing with anticipation. I expect her lips to meet mine, but a cool spoon touches my mouth, delivering a silky, soft bite. The incredible smooth spoonful is a flavor burst—salty, greasy, and sweet. I savor the astonishing taste. My eyes involuntarily open, and my tongue lets the bite sit and melt.

"Mmmmmm. What is it?" I ask.

Mary's gaze holds mine—her eyes filled with warmth. "You are enjoying our traditional dish, Eskimo ice cream, made with muktuk, akutaq, and berries. It's delicate and complex. I think it encapsulates our culture in one bite."

I hold Mary's gaze, my simmering eyes mirroring the moment's sweet intensity.

"Delicious and unexpected. I agree." I murmur, my voice thick with desire for her.

Chapter 18

Elder Mary

The last villagers are vaccinated, and Riley and I are in her makeshift flu clinic, aka my cozy bedroom.

My heart races as Riley gazes at me, licking the Eskimo ice cream from her lips. She tenderly places the spoon down on the desk before gently turning to me and looking into my eyes, her lips part, and she slowly leans into me. Our lips meet at last.

My breath quickens as her soft lips brush mine to share a tender ice cream–sweetened kiss. I thought about her lips on mine since first seeing her on the airfield. She dazzled me with her emotions, a contained rage at Trevor, and her awe at seeing our beautiful village landscape for the first time.

Her beauty only increased when her expression fluttered through her array of emotions and settled into a warm and inviting smile, lighting up her face and leaving me breathless when she looked at me for our first greeting.

I circle my arms around her body as she melts into me. The kiss is even better than I imagined. It is a velvety swirl of smooth ice cream melting blissfully on her tongue. I'm lost in the moment, completely swept away by our first kiss and the emotional wave it causes within me.

Looking at her delicate neck, I'm debating between moving Riley to my bed to taste more of her. My luxurious fur blankets look rather comfy, but in the back of my mind, I know I need to stop because of my role as a respected village elder and my Yup'ik people's representative. Kissing the government nurse is totally unacceptable, and my village is on the other side of my bedroom door, probably waiting to congratulate Riley on her flu clinic.

My heart and mind wage a battle, passionately struggling and igniting my spirit with a rush I hardly recognize. Her beauty and kindness captivate me, and her kiss pulls me into a wild riptide.

The reality of being an elder crashes into me like the winter waves to the shore. Indulging in a romantic relationship with an outsider is frowned upon and blurs the professional boundaries I model and uphold for the village. I must stop before this spirals into a catastrophic situation.

The knock at the door interrupts our moment and thankfully stops the kiss for me. Gary's voice seeps through the door, "Hey, can I come in?"

I lean away from Riley, catching my breath, and before I say anything, Gary walks in.

Riley averts her gaze and turns away her flushed rosy hued cheeks, delicately gathering her medical supplies. I hear her heart pounding even as she calmly arranges her supplies.

"Umph," Gary says, scowling at me. "Trevor's calling on the radio for you."

I nod, grateful yet disappointed for his interruption. I smile at Riley, stand, and walk to the kitchen to take the call on the CB radio. My mind reels from the kiss, questioning whether I can ignore my connection with her, even with my brother and a cabin full of people, to reinforce my decision not to get romantically involved with an outsider.

"Thank you for your help," I hear Riley say to my brother.

"My pleasure, Nurse. The kids at the school appreciate the time and attention you showed them at lunch. If you decide to come back," he says gruffly, "maybe you can teach a curriculum health lesson. I don't really enjoy teaching the sexual health unit."

I'm surprised Gary's considering letting an outsider teach and the possibility of her coming back. He distrusts outsiders intensely. His invitation for her to return is a big step in accepting an outsider's help.

I hear her agreeing and asking him to send her the lesson plan he usually follows for the sex ed unit.

Excellent! Riley is planning to return to Portlock, and I might need to sit in on her class to get a refresher on sex ed. It's been a few years since my high school health education, and an elder should sit in and see what our children are learning.

I radio back, "This is Mary at Portlock, over."

Trevor says loud and clear, cutting through the village party noise, "I'll be rescuing my girlfriend from your shithole in twenty minutes."

"Copy that. Landing in twenty," I grit my teeth to remain professional as I radio back.

The words hit me, a blow, shattering the fragile hope blossoming. *Girlfriend* is the one that stings most.

Did I misinterpret Riley's signals and overestimate our shared connection? She is actually with Trevor. He did have his arm practically around her when I drove up to his plane on the airfield. Perhaps a lovers' quarrel caused the tension I felt there. I didn't ask Riley if she was single or exactly why she was so angry with Trevor.

I am a fool and entirely out of practice with dating. I believe we share the same feelings, but she's a gorgeous city girl who probably kisses a different person every weekend.

The teenagers, hearing the radio exchange, spring into action. They take the medical boxes from Riley and load them onto my truck outside.

I put on my boots and jacket, then turn to fetch Riley. But she's right behind me, zipping up her pink coat and putting on her cold-weather gear from her bags.

I hand her my parka, knowing the wind will cut through her city puffer jacket. She needs an authentic parka to keep her warm and remind her of our tender kiss. "Keep mine. You'll need a warm jacket for your next village trip."

"I couldn't. . ." she says, forgetting my lesson on graciously receiving villager gifts.

"You can and *will*. I am not having our village nurse freeze to death and I will sew and bead another parka this winter. What else is there to do on our long dark winter nights?"

My brain says, *except for kissing you*, giving me another image of her wrapped tightly in my arms in front of my cozy wood stove.

"Thank you. I'm honored," Riley says graciously, ducking her head and wrapping herself in my parka.

She slowly circles the room, ensuring everyone receives personal goodbyes, and no one feels faint after the flu clinic. She holds baby Moe's hand to wave with him as Gary sidles up next to me and whispers in my ear.

"Don't even consider it, Bob. Your feelings are written across your face." He adds, "She's nice, but don't trust outsiders. City people come and go; only the villagers stay. I don't want you to get hurt."

"I'm thinking the same," I reply, willing my heart and brain to agree with my brother. But they tell me a different story, throwing my heart back into the unpredictable riptide of my emotions.

I must protect myself and my village!

Chapter 19

Nurse Riley

Dread washes over me as Trevor's announcement of me being his "girlfriend" and calling their home a "shithole" echoes through the radio. I enjoyed my visit, making me forget about him and my flight home. If only a different pilot could fly me back from Portlock to Anchorage, I wouldn't need to deal with him again.

The thought of spending another hour enduring his unwanted flirting fills me with disgust. I shake my head, trying to erase the memory of his repulsive touch.

Gary's questioning stare draws my attention, forcing me to focus on the conversation. He asked about my teaching at the school, and I respond, trying to maintain my composure despite my stormy emotions raging within. My heart drums against my calm facade, threatening to expose my inner turmoil.

"Of course, I'd love to help, and I'll bring more information about the University of Anchorage for your three graduating seniors. Stacy has her nursing scholarship, but there's a diesel mechanics program Peter might be interested in applying to. Also, Ellen will love the online small business courses, if she wants to do coursework from here. With her experience in her fur business she won't have any problems," I surmise. My heart continues furiously attacking me as I try to maintain my calm.

How am I going to survive another flight with the cocky Bush Pilot?

The joy from the successful flu clinic and my village trip quickly fades as I mentally prepare for the journey home. I hurriedly finish packing, letting the eager students carry the boxes and propel me to the door.

I manage to say and wave my goodbyes to each villager, who hug and wish me a safe trip home. These villagers, strangers hours ago, are hugging me as if I'm family and talking about my next visit. Waving with baby Moe makes my eyes tear up.

Stacy says, "Thanks again for teaching and inspiring me. Have a nice trip to the airport with Bob." She slyly winks at me, sending a heat wave rippling across my cheeks.

Since Stacy is obviously referring to me starting a relationship with Mary, perhaps no one noticed Trevor calling me his girlfriend. They are probably used to his rudeness.

Stacy adds, "Trevor is cute but Bob is the best. I'd pick Bob any day of the week."

Ugh! Nevermind. Does Mary think I lied to her and I am dating Trevor? I hope she doesn't believe that and doesn't hate me.

Mary avoids asking me about it and places her fancy, hand-beaded parka into my hands. The heat returns to my cheeks. This is a special parka, and I couldn't accept the gift, but she won't take no for an answer.

She firmly tells me to take it in front of everyone, and I can't refuse. I look at the wood stove, imagining her sitting in front of the warm glow, beading a new parka, and drinking hot chocolate this winter.

I pitied the villagers' quiet, non-Starbucks life. But, I am jealous of her winter plans, and I wish I were sitting beside her, reading a book and drinking her sweet hot chocolate as she beads. Surrounded by friends, this tranquil Alaskan village is a warm and vibrant place.

I smile with a dreamy expression thinking about how my ideas shifted, and the villagers' attitude toward me changed too. Not one person referred to me as a Cheechako or outsider tonight. They welcomed and invited me back, just as I had hoped for on my first village visit.

However, my departure snaps me back to the present. Following Mary's lead, I hasten my steps toward the dark truck. The moon replaces the sun, casting an eerie glow over the tundra, amplifying my heightened emotions. Darkness and my upcoming flight with Trevor unsettle me, while Mary's once-welcoming demeanor is now icy and professional.

As soon as she unlocks it, she gets in without glancing back at me. I want to explain. I enjoyed her kiss, and Trevor is *not* my boyfriend. But the scowl on her face kills the opportunity to talk. Clenching my fists in frustration, I open the passenger side door and throw myself into the seat.

Even though this nursing trip is a success, I'm disappointed. I open my mouth, struggling to form the words to repair our relationship. *But what is our relationship, anyway?* I'm a government employee assigned to their village, and she is one of the village's gatekeepers. I realize Mary and I will never be in a romantic relationship, even without Trevor's comment.

"Thank you for your help and support," the words slip from my lips, genuine appreciation mixed with regret. Without her encouragement and village connections, my job would be in jeopardy.

Mary nods in response, her gaze fixed outside, lost in thought. "Let's enjoy this quiet night," she remarks.

I remain silent, respecting her contemplative mood. Her demeanor mirrors the cold and impenetrable tundra beyond my window.

Uncomfortable silence engulfs us as we drive the remaining distance to the airport. When we finally arrive at the Quonset hut, Mary breaks the silence, exiting the truck and offering, "I am sorry about what happened in the bedroom. Let's forget about it. I didn't realize you and Trevor were together."

The words catch me off guard. "What?" I croak as she shuts the door, and I hurry to get out of the Bronco.

Chapter 20

Nurse Riley

"I am most definitely not with Trevor!" I assert, jumping out of the car and yelling it to Mary's back. "He's obnoxious, and I'm terrified of getting back on a plane with him." I pull my hands from my pockets, showing Mary how they shake.

Mary's expression softens, "I'm sorry!" She walks to me and holds my hands. "Trevor called you his girlfriend and he was hugging you this morning. It kinda made sense."

Embarrassment and confusion flushes my cheeks as to why Mary would believe I'd be with someone like him. "Trevor lied. He called me 'sweetheart' throughout the entire flight. He had no right to harass me or touch me," I say, crossing my arms protectively and jutting my chin in defiance.

"I apologize. You don't deserve anyone disrespecting you, and, without question, Trevor should not touch you," she murmurs. Her eyes flash, and she holds my hands tighter.

"Thank you. I'm not upset with you. I've gotta sit, trapped next to him, for the hour flight home." I respond while I shake my head. "I'm sure he will be the douchebag he was on the flight here," I add. "And he almost killed me too."

She nods with understanding. "I must admit, I'm relieved to hear that you're not with Trevor, and not just because he's a jerk," she says, her gaze meeting mine from beneath her long, dark lashes. She gives me a shrug and a sideways smile without saying anything more.

Her words stun me. *Is Mary admitting her feelings for me?*

"Trevor is a jerk. He purposely didn't unload my medical supplies because I wasn't fawning over him and the size of his car," I huff back.

She chuckles, her laughter breaking the icy tension between us. "Fawning over his car size? I hope that's not a euphemism for something else," she teases.

I smile back, the joke making us both smile as she continues holding my hands, coming closer to me.

"No. I mean Trevor's actual car. He showed me cell phone pictures of his sports car to impress me and was trying to get a date with me."

"Better than him showing you pictures of . . ." Mary laughs and pulls me to her, planting a delicate kiss over my smile.

Mary's lips are warm and light. She smells invitingly of campfire smoke, a subtle reminder of the warmth of her woodfired cabin. Her gentle lips taste sweet, igniting the desire inside me. Her solid body is warm, and I wrap my arms around her and move closer to connect with her as we kiss.

My emotions for Mary are intensifying with each passing second. Despite our differences, I'm enamored with her strength, captivated by her gentle kiss. I am a white, city nurse, and Mary is a respected village elder. Our backgrounds, lifestyles, and cultures are opposite. But there's an intangible spark between us neither of us can resist.

Opposites attract, which is proving to be true. My pinned hair, starched shirt, and pink stained lips mingle with her raven hair, fur parka, and wide mouth to match perfectly.

Mary's quiet confidence and inherent strength commands respect and exudes a calming influence. She earned the school children's regard, and her people honored her as an elder. And she deserves someone as strong as her, not a new nurse who has a panic attack on her first day in the village.

After a moment, I reluctantly untangle my arms from her and pull my face away.

"I didn't even need to show you the size of my car," Mary says with a playful wink.

I unwittingly smile back at her. "That's only because I'm by your oversized pick-up," I point out breathlessly.

"Does this mean you are single?" Mary inquires, her voice lilting a hopeful note.

"Mary, I wouldn't have kissed you if I wasn't," I say, my voice raising. Then I add, "But this - us- is a terrible idea." I'm totally wrong for her, and she is one of my village patients.

Mary runs her hand over her face and nods before I can further explain. "You are right. I can't be the representative for my village, fighting for the government to recognize my people's rights and our traditions and be with a . . ."

The icy tension returns, blowing away our warm kiss and leaving me shaking my head at her words, raining on me like sleet. "You mean a white city girl who looks like Barbie? Or do you mean a government employee?" I pause, my heart pounding, "Or maybe you mean a *cheechako* outsider?"

She moves away from me, creating distance between us. "I didn't mean any of those. This isn't about you. I represent my entire village and tribe. My decision's impacts are huge, which means, I need to carefully consider my actions, as an elder."

I avert my gaze, my eyes welling with tears. She doesn't correct my assumptions, I notice. She still sees me as a cheechako - a clueless, uncaring outsider. Here

I was, daydreaming about spending a winter with her, by the fire, and she didn't even believe I would return or that I could survive in Portlock.

Bitterly, I retort, "I can't date patients anyway."

She nods, agreeing with my decision mirroring hers.

I immediately regret the coldness between us and a lump forms in my throat. I don't want to leave Mary and our last kiss like this. But this is for the best. Long-distance relationships and opposites do not end in a happily ever after. My heart thunders in my ears, a pounding beat telling me to say *something.*

Before I can apologize for my hurtful words, Mary speaks, "I'm a village elder, and you're a city nurse. We are oil and water." She turns and strides toward the hangar to prepare for the plane's arrival.

As I shut the open truck door, the airstrip lights flicker on, and Mary's warm parka protects me from the chill surrounding me. The beautiful parka is a reminder of her warm, tender kiss and protective embrace.

Chapter 21

Elder Mary

My anger simmers as I wait at the airport for Trevor to arrive and transport Riley back home. The situation with her is maddening. First, she kisses me and then says she doesn't want a relationship. Our day is a whirlwind of mixed signals and frustrations.

I glance at her, sitting in my leather chair and engrossed, scrolling on her phone. I'm unusually irritated. *Outsiders are always on their phones, oblivious to their surroundings – city people possess no sense of connection or appreciation for the world around them.*

The radio crackle interrupts my thoughts, signaling Trevor's imminent arrival. I brace myself for his obnoxious presence, another urbanite who disrespects our village.

Riley sets down her phone, hearing the roaring Bush plane landing outside.

"Your ride is here," I gesture to the door, while I bring my truck keys to drive her luggage to the plane.

We step outside together and watch Trevor exiting the plane, falling headfirst from the window, then standing unsteadily and holding the wing for balance. My frustration deepens as I realize his condition. *How did he even manage to fly here?*

Riley gasps.

Trevor is drunk.

"Hey, over here!" He hollers, beaming and flapping his arms – a madman alone on the airstrip.

We approach Trevor, and the pungent alcohol stench assaults us. He is undeniably drunk. I shake my head, infuriated by his recklessness.

"Heyyyyy!" Trevor slurs, oblivious to our concern, as he stumbles toward the airport entrance. We follow him inside, witnessing his collision with a table and the shattering of a coffee mug that rolls off.

"Wherz te cofftee?" he demands, his speech slurred.

"It's going to take more than coffee to sober you up," I retort, bending to clean the mug's broken pieces.

Trevor ignores my comment, collapsing into a chair with a suggestive wink at Riley. "Girlfrrrrien, ya ready?"

Riley turns to me with wide eyes, her mouth open but no words escaping. Her anxiety and worry are palpable.

Before she speaks, he gestures toward me and continues, "Native, load the bags. Te importantz people or leavfing." Then, he burps.

I shake my head. *This is a rare moment that I wish we were in a big city airport with security and police.* He's plastered. I don't know how he managed to fly here or what village bar let him leave. There's no way he'd pass a breathalyzer test to fly legally.

"I can't fly with him," Riley whispers to me.

Her breathing increases, and I touch her hand to calm her. I respond, "No one is flying with him. I'll call our Village Security Officer, Pete."

"Whadda you two whispering about, and where's my damn coffee," Trevor yells, shutting his eyes and scratching himself.

"How will I get home?" Riley asks me, her voice an octave high.

"I'll figure it out. Let me take care of this first." I walk over to the radio and call Pete to the airport, then step back and start a pot of coffee.

I'm making it for Pete, not for this idiot.

"Come onz. Ive a sayzdule. Hurrzzy up," Trevor says, resting his chin on his chest, eyes glued shut.

"You aren't flying tonight. You are sleeping it off here," I tell him.

His eyes blaze open. "I fint," he mumbles as he attempts to stand from the chair and fails before his butt rises. His body falls further back from the effort.

"You can't even open your eyes. Take a nap," I tell Trevor.

"Will you let him fly later?" She asks.

"No. He's not going anywhere but to Anchorage in handcuffs tomorrow," I explain in a hushed tone. Not that it matters, as he is suddenly asleep with drool dripping from his mouth.

"But I need to get home tonight. There's nowhere to stay, and he's the only pilot." She looks around wildly, her breathing dramatically increases.

Not wanting another panic attack, I grab her hands. "Slow your breathing. 1-2-3 in and 1-2-3 out." I model, taking a deep breath with her as I look into her wide eyes.

"We keep another pilot hidden in the village. He's excellent. I'll get him coffee, and he'll be fine for the one-hour flight to Anchorage," I say, soothing her with my steady voice.

The coffee pot beeps as the coffee starts dripping out, and she's distracted. Her breathing slows to a regular pace.

"Okay," she responds.

I take stock of the situation and radio Gary to assist at the airport. It will be better to retain additional help if Trevor wakes and becomes belligerent.

"Roger that. I'll come with Pete. He's grabbing an extra food plate from the party to bring. Over," Gary radios back.

Knowing I called him to the airport, Pete assumes he will hang out for a while since there are no flights to Anchorage until tomorrow. Transporting unruly outsiders back to the city is a common task for him.

My anger at Riley is gone and replaced with tenderness. I check to ensure her breathing is slow and another panic attack isn't imminent. I can't imagine the hellish trip she endured with Trevor on the way to the village, but there's no way I am letting her risk getting into a plane with him drunk.

I realize I care about Riley—It's more than wanting her safe.

"Is Gary flying me home, then?" Riley asks, catching my eye.

I take a deep breath and assure her, "I'm taking you home."

And at the moment, as our eyes meet, I recognize our intimate connection. I care deeply for her, and I will keep her safe. No matter what lies ahead, I'm willing to face my brother and any other villager who challenges me to see her again and to hold her in my protective embrace.

Chapter 22

Nurse Riley

My heart dances while heat courses through me at Mary's mention of taking me home. Despite telling her I wanted to keep our relationship professional, my mind flashes to snuggling with her, the woodstove flickering, and a mug of sweet hot chocolate in my hand.

"I'm flying you home. I am an excellent pilot. I'll go get my plane ready," she says to my surprise. My smile falters. Mary's words dash my romantic daydream of returning to her cabin with her and disregarding our mutual agreement at our relationship's impossibility.

Misinterpreting my frown, Mary explains, "I'm a qualified pilot, and I fly to Anchorage weekly. You'll be safe with me."

I nod, acknowledging her words while suppressing my desire for something more. I need to apologize for my harsh words and clarify I want to maintain a professional connection with her. Losing her friendship is the last thing I want, but I'm not ready to navigate what a professional relationship with her would look like. *Can working professionals hug? Hold hands? Kiss?*

Trevor's disruptive snort draws our attention to his drunken state. Mary and I exchange an exasperated look.

"Thank you for. . ." I point to Trevor.

Mary nods, her lips pressed together.

The door opens with a whoosh, and Gary and Pete enter, stomping off their boots and carrying enough food for five men.

"What's going on, Boss?" Pete asks Mary.

Trevor, awakened by the commotion, clumsily gets up from his chair. "Wev are loadin upz. Come on!"

I look at Mary with my brows raised.

"Here. Drink a cup of coffee," she says, handing Trevor a freshly-brewed coffee to distract him.

I walk alongside Mary to greet the newcomers, eager to avoid being alone with Trevor and his incoherent rambling.

"Trevor is stinking drunk, and we need to keep an eye on him to keep him from flying tonight," Mary summarizes, pointing to Trevor, whose body is draped over a coat rack to stay standing while concentrating on getting the coffee cup to his mouth. He hits the coffee against his ear and curses.

Pete tilts his head. "Got it. We'll stay and monitor *this* situation until morning. Then the Alaska State Troopers can fly in to take our drunk and disorderly to Anchorage." He settles into the leather chair by the desk.

Trevor slurs, "Donut, you guyzz has sumtin to add to tis?" He stumbles a few steps toward us with a grin plastered on his face. He sways, and his bloodshot eyes move to me. "I could uss a naughty nurzz."

I ignore his rude comment and his wink. I would comment back, but I won't waste my breath. In his current state, he won't remember anything I say.

He moves to the wall and slumps against it.

I'm relieved he is safely immobile, but I do need to apologize to Mary without the audience. *I'll wait until we are on the plane.*

Mary takes charge. "I'll fire up the plane to take Riley to Anchorage and leave you in charge here," she says to Pete and Gary.

They nod as she walks out, settling into chairs, nibbling on their food, and pulling out playing cards.

Trevor loses his balance, toppling to the floor and spilling the coffee down the wall. No one moves to assist him as he curls onto his side and immediately falls back into a snoring sleep.

"Bob's a great pilot. You'll get home fine," Pete says with a wave.

Gary nods at me.

"Thanks for the party," Pete says, "I hardly felt my flu shot."

I mumble a soft "You're welcome" under my breath, my tiredness from the hectic day seeping into my voice.

Desperate for a pick-me-up, I grab a steaming coffee, add plenty of sugar, and grab Mary's cup for her.

Gary points at the window, telling me, "Bob is ready. You should head out."

I tuck the parka around myself and avoid snoring Trevor's splayed legs to walk out to meet Mary and the plane.

Seeing me, she opens the little side door. With her assisting me, I climb inside, noticing my secured medical supplies. The plane itself is tidy and well-organized. I sit next to her and put on the familiar sound-blocking radio headset.

She straps herself into her seat and shows me with her seatbelt how to click in the five-point harness around me, then tells me over the headset, "I need to do a quick check and calculate the weight. Give me a minute."

I pull the parka tighter around myself. The soft fur engulfs my face and neck. Watching Mary working through her preflight checklist, checking the gauges, and recording numbers give me confidence in her skills, not to mention she is sexy as hell in a cockpit. As a pilot, she exudes even more confidence, which is super-hot.

"How much do you weigh?" she asks with a note of apology in her voice.

"135," I say, "And about seventy-five pounds in medical supplies."

Mary jots down the numbers, focusing solely on the task at hand. Meanwhile, my mind wanders, envisioning my weight sitting on her lap, kissing her passionately.

I scold myself, realizing I need to stay focused and take this opportunity to apologize. I wait for her to finish the sheet and power us down the runway and into the air, easily piloting the plane.

Once in the air and steady, I tell her, "I actually think the home office assumed the villagers would refuse my flu vaccinations today, which is why they didn't pack regular bandaids. The Barbie ones are probably left over from the last nurse."

Mary smiles and replies, "I actually like the Barbie bandaids. They're memorable, especially when you put one on Gary."

Her words bring forth a genuine laugh, momentarily distracting me from the turbulent thoughts bouncing around, and then the plane bounces. I grab Mary's leg involuntarily, recalling the terrifying moment when the aircraft veered towards the river.

She covers my hand tenderly just as a serene tranquility washes over me. Her touch comforts me. In her soothing, confident voice, which I fell in love with on the flight over, she says, "We are alright."

Chapter 23

Elder Mary

Riley's delicate hand rests on my thigh, igniting a fire within me. Unable to resist, I cover her hand with mine, savoring her warm and tender touch. Even the universe is urging us to confront our deepening connection.

I reassure her, and my nerves fire throughout my body, sparking my imagination.

What if we could be together? What if I could kiss her soft lips again and feel her happy sighs?

"I enjoyed your visit. Did Portlock meet your expectations?" I ask, hoping to make an opportunity to tell her my feelings.

Her gaze locks with mine, and she breathes, "I loved it. I can't thank you enough for saving me and my clinic." A shy giggle escapes her lips, and her cheeks flush with a rosy hue.

"It's my pleasure. You are a capable and caring nurse. Even without me, you'd be a success. I'm happy to help," I reply with sincerity.

"I want to see you again. Can I take you to breakfast tomorrow?" I ask, taking advantage of the tender atmosphere and her hand resting on my leg. Despite our different backgrounds and lifestyles, I find myself falling for her.

She hesitates for a moment, her thoughts racing. "I… I want to see you too," she finally confesses, her voice filled with vulnerability.

She's not from our village, she doesn't lead the same life we do, and yet, I cannot deny the love blossoming within me. I'm captivated by her warm blue eyes and how she nervously chats. Her care for Portlock's people, her willingness to learn and respect our traditions, and her genuine kindness is sexy and attractive. The villagers, from the students to the elders, sense it too, accepting and trusting her as our village nurse.

Also, I miss having someone to love. All my focus has been on the village.

The realization hits me hard—I can't let her slip away and disappear from my life. I am falling—or am I actually— *in love* with this outsider. My heart is open and there's no way to close it, I will not let her go and risk not seeing her again.

Silently, we gaze out the window at the starry sky, lost in our thoughts. Perhaps she's thinking about our shared kiss, and I wish she would tell me her feelings. I want to say something, but the enjoyment of the beautiful stars tells me nature is showing us how perfect we are for each other.

"You've helped me immensely, but I won't risk my career dating a patient," she finally says, her eyes averted though her hand remains intertwined with mine resting on my thigh.

Riley's words sting, but I understand her position. However, I am going to fight for her. She might not realize we are a perfect fit, but there's no one else for me.

"Riley, you work for the State of Alaska. Isn't every Alaskan your patient? Don't you deserve someone to care for you the way you care for others?" I counter, searching for a way to bridge the gap between us.

Her eyes meet mine, shimmering with unshed tears. "I can't. I am following a plan, and as a new village nurse, I need to focus on work and gain seniority. Then maybe, after I hit my goals in a few years, I will start dating."

"I didn't plan on falling for an outsider, but fate brought us together for a reason. I'm here to help you with your village nursing plan and you are here to teach me that I don't *have to* be alone," I explain, my thumb caressing her hand gently. As much as I love flying my Beaver plane, I long to be on solid ground, to hold her in my arms as we talk.

"You're a patient," she weakly insists, her voice filled with uncertainty.

"I'm not your patient. Today, I'm your friend, flying you home," I declare, determination lacing my words.

Riley's expression shifts, and she suddenly grabs her folder. She lets go of my hand to thumb through it. "Wait, why aren't you on my village patient list?"

A smile tugs at my lips. "I live in Anchorage and work for the tribe there. I'm covering the airport for Moe's mom. She is spending time bonding with him. I love my home in Portlock and helping out. I enjoy visits to my family and spending time in my cozy cabin there."

She nods. "I see. So, you *aren't* my village patient. I still need to protect you from the flu. You've done an extreme amount to help me. The least I can do is keep you healthy."

"How about we schedule my flu shot tomorrow morning over breakfast?" I suggest.

"Here's a better idea, why don't I take you to the clinic and put on your Barbie band-aid. And then we get breakfast," Riley counters, smiling.

"You are oddly excited to see me get a flu shot," I observe as I capture her finger and lightly kiss it. "What if I told you, I'm afraid of needles?"

"I don't believe anything scares you, Mary. But I'm going as your friend, not your nurse," she says, brushing her fingertips lightly over the traditional lines on my chin.

"I could say the same for you. Not many people can pull a jar off a feral cat or convince my brother to invite an outsider back to our village. You are pretty damn fearless," I express.

She blushes, "Then Mary, let's have a date. I want to see you," she says shyly.

"It's a plan—"

Suddenly, as if on cue, a breathtaking display unfolds before us. Dazzling lights dance gracefully across the sky, painting vivid green and fading yellow hues. The magical Aurora Borealis, my ancestors watching over us, unravels across the sky all around us.

Gasping in awe, Riley's voice fills my headset. We enjoy front-row seats to the greens and blues twisting and surrounding the plane. The Northern Lights hypnotize us with their beauty. In a state of peaceful wonder, we hold hands and marvel at nature's ethereal symphony. With her hand firmly tucked into mine, we share the intimate moment, our hearts in perfect harmony, under the celestial lights.

Get ready to get trapped in a Christmas Eve blizzard as the storm rages outside, the two women, Makayla and Pauline, must fight for survival while grappling with the emotional storms brewing inside in

Wilderness Rescue: Unthaw My Heart.

Available Now.

Discover the books in the *Wilderness Rescue* series by continuing the journey at HarmonyNoble.com.

Keep reading to enjoy the next book.

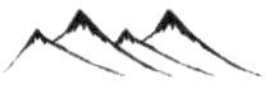

Wilderness Rescue: Unthaw My Heart
Chapter 1: Makayla (aka Mak)

SNOW CHAINS REQUIRED.

My attention snaps from the mesmerizing white landscape to the road sign illuminated by my Jeep's headlights.

The powdery snow flits lazily across my windshield, a whirling dance, as my tires carve a deep path through the snow-covered road. On Christmas Eve, the daylight is fading early at four in the afternoon. The tranquil, remote Caribou Hills is silent and frosty.

Buzz. Buzz. Buzz.

I glance at my phone in my cup holder, trying to get my attention with the glowing, vibrating ringing. It's another call from Bryant, my ex-fiancé, trying to convince me not to go to the cabin alone. But as soon as my eyes dart back to the road, they widen, my muscles tense, and my hands squeeze the steering wheel as I crest an icy slope. The tires lose their grip, floating over the road, and my knuckles turn white, clenching the steering wheel that no longer controls my Jeep.

"No! No! Not now!" I cry futilely. My stomach moves to my throat, suffocating me, and my left hand reflexively moves to cover the Saint Michael's medallion at my throat.

My car is in an icy, downhill freefall, and I can't stop it as I careen down the steep slope. My breathing shallow, I yank the steering wheel following the direction of the slide, praying for traction. Miraculously, the tires catch before I enter the deep ditch, allowing me to wrestle back control from the icy road.

I mutter a prayer of thanks, but the tires skate again, not responding to my direction. I desperately try to steer back onto the road, but the laws of physics are working against me. In a cruel twist of fate, the Jeep gains speed, skating faster down the hill as if it's building up momentum for a triple axel instead of slowing for the corner.

"Oh God!"

In sheer panic, my foot slams down the brake pedal, my final attempt to regain control and stop the slide. Instead, the Jeep gives me a bone-jarring jolt, veering off the road and the snowy ditch, unable to stop its speed as it *whooshes* and *thumps,* making me squeeze my eyes shut.

Being unable to stop my Jeep from throwing me into the surrounding dark woods is worse than nicking an artery during surgery—at least an artery can be clamped and repaired. I'm powerless to the disorderly elements, and I'm without my hospital team to help.

Thump.

My breath hitches as the Jeep suddenly stops, jerking my body forward. I open my eyes to the blurry snow and darkness outside my windshield. My hands remain locked on the wheel as adrenaline shoots through me like an electric shock—my heart pounds. My lungs ache for air. My hands are clenched and shaking from my close call.

The adrenaline hits my brain, allowing me to process the situation and shift into my emergency room autopilot.

Gingerly peeling my fingers from the steering wheel, one by one, I check that each of my digits is functional. I'm uninjured but can't stay in the Jeep, as no one will see me this far off the road. I look at my phone- *no signal* and my gaze drifts upward, landing on the road thirty feet away. My stomach churns as my brain processes the harsh reality. Between the deep snow and the distance uphill, there's no way my Jeep is getting back to the road.

And who knows when anyone else will be driving down this remote road. I don't have any snow gear, food, or water because I dropped everything off at the cabin days ago for my annual Christmas Eve holiday. This is my first year without my parents, and I plan to enjoy a quiet, cozy holiday-just me with a sweet romance novel and hot chocolate in front of the fire.

My cabin isn't too far, and the snow is increasing. I must leave immediately before whiteout conditions hit, or navigating there will be impossible.

I'm hiking through the snow to the cabin.

I change the gear into park, and the engine's low hum is the only sound in the eerie stillness. Shaking, I turn off the Jeep, cutting off the engine noise.

"Dear Lord, give me strength," I whisper, tucking my holiday hat over my head and zipping up my woefully thin jacket.

Opening the door, the wind and icy snow slap my face, and I tug the Santa hat further down as my boots crunch against the unforgiving ice, a bleak soundtrack to the frozen challenge of walking back to the road and then to my cabin.

Teeth chattering, I trudge onward, a lone figure walking in the biting cold. Every breath creates an icy halo around me. Trying to stay calm, I wrap my arms around my shivering body, attempting to preserve my heat. My fingers are frozen sausages, aching with the cold, and only the garish Santa cap shields me from the biting wind.

I berate myself for this unlucky situation. *Why? Why didn't I take the time to ensure I had my winter chains in my Jeep?*

The thought of an Alaskan Emergency Room doctor freezing to death on Christmas Eve in a blizzard is absurd—*Impossible!* And someone discovering me on Christmas, frozen solid in my cheesy Santa hat, makes me want to throw the hat into the woods. But I like my ears, and frostbite is no joke.

My plan was to be nestled warm in my cabin for the holiday, far from the chaos of work and the fresh wounds of my recent breakup with Bryant. Instead, I'm slogging through knee-deep snow, battling an unexpected Alaskan blizzard.

"Time to check for a signal," I mutter aloud. The sound of my voice solidifies my resolve as I trudge onward.

And there *it* is, the last message from Bryant lighting up my phone screen. *Call me if you need anything. I'll come out there and join you, Mak Attack.*

The words hang in the air, my mind playing them on a loop, and I yell at the useless *phone, him, the blizzard.* "I'm *stranded.* No one can find me! Bryant, I wouldn't call you *if* I had cell reception. *I DON'T LOVE YOU!"*

The snow muffles the words as it obscures the moon and starlight. My cheeks flush with embarrassment as I replay the disappointment clouding Bryant's face when I ended our engagement weeks ago and his desperate attempts to convince me that "love grows from friendship" and I needed to "give *us* more time."

However, the truth is, *my heart is telling me Bryant isn't the one.* Freezing to death is karma's way of punishing me for shattering a man's heart who did nothing wrong but love the wrong woman.

With each freezing step into the wind, I'm kicking myself for my poor clothing choice. Jeans were an unfortunate decision, and my feet should be warm in wool socks, not my thin cotton work socks. The Alaskan winter is unforgiving and doesn't care about my cold feet and misery.

Adding to my regrets, I didn't check that my snow chains were in the Jeep when I rushed out of the house. And confounding my misfortune, I didn't stop at the Ninilchik gas station to put on the chains before going off-road. If I had, I would have realized I didn't have them and bought another pair to put on the Jeep. The gas station attendant might even have warned me about the weather, and I wouldn't be in this predicament.

No one but Bryant, hours away in Anchorage, even knows I'm out here.

I clap my hands together to get the blood flowing.

Why did I bolt without snow gear and chains? I'm Alaskan AND a doctor—I should know better!

In any other place, calling Roadside Assistance would be a no-brainer. But here, miles from civilization, with no cell service and zero chance of a tow truck locating me. I'm an idiot for not using snow chains and my stupid clothing choice.

Still, I bite my dry bottom lip and tightly smile to maintain my optimism. *At least I'm able to walk rather than being crushed inside my crashed Jeep.* In Alaska, danger lurks in every pristine snowdrift, as I know from working in Emergency Medicine.

I'm alive, walking, and I will make it to my cabin.

The wind howls around me, cutting through my clothing.

Why didn't I pack my snow gear? Why didn't I bring a thermos of hot chocolate?

My thoughts spiral negatively, but the thoughts distract me from an even bleaker possibility—succumbing to hypothermia and dying alone in this relentless snowstorm.

And why don't I love my handsome fiancé, Bryant? That's the million-dollar question I ask myself too many times and can't seem to answer.

He cares about me and wants me to spend the holidays with him, not at the cabin. And if I'd have shown him any kindness and asked before rushing out of the house, he would've put the snow chains on the Jeep.

The scene, hours old, plays out in my mind. Coming home from work, I planned to shower and dress, then head to my parents' cabin. But Bryant was home, lingering, trying to talk me out of going, to instead stay home with him and make a new holiday tradition.

I don't need a new tradition! Also, I'm not marrying him, so he will *not* be part of my upcoming holiday traditions.

He hasn't moved out, and he's not accepting the break-up well despite me bluntly sharing my feelings with him.

We haven't officially announced our breakup to our coworkers. So, on top of being exhausted from a shift at the hospital, where all my coworkers wished me a Merry Christmas with my new fiancé, I have to find the energy to tell him, *again,* that I'm not *marrying him* and forcefully eject him from our home.

Our hospital schedules are chaotic at St Mary's Alaska Medical Center, where we work, and this cabin trip was supposed to give me some much-needed space and time to reflect. But Bryant ignored my plans.

He lit candles and baked Shepherd's Pie when I arrived home. I had hoped he'd pack his things and move out before Christmas, but he's attempting to rekindle our nonexistent love.

His voice echoes, "Mak, can't you see I'm perfect for you? We're getting married, and we work together. Your parents approved of us! You are ruining a perfect relationship. What will everyone think when you tell them you're dumping me?"

I didn't argue—I fled my house and Bryant's dinner for the cabin. I have everything I need at the Caribou Hills cabin. Moreover, *I need to be alone.*

That was my first mistake!

Why did I let his arguments bother me? Why can't I get him to accept we are no longer together, and he'd be better off with anyone but me? I cannot marry someone I don't love!

Since my parents' funeral, we haven't been happy. *Really, we weren't jolly before, either.* Their sudden death made me reevaluate my life and my happiness. Instead of clinging to Bryant for support, I found myself pushing him away, realizing that just because he is perfect on paper, attending the same church, working with me, having similar hobbies, and having my parents' approval, it didn't mean he was the right person for me.

If he's my soulmate, why am I so unhappy when we are together?

Our interactions are tense and resentful, with him trying too hard to be friendly and irritating me. It's a cycle of dating, fighting, apologizing, and dating again. We are functional at work, in the chaos of the Emergency Room. But our relationship crumbles outside St Mary's, and we aren't even friendly roommates anymore, giving each other the silent treatment, driving separately to work, and sleeping in different rooms.

To be fair, we've *always* slept in separate rooms because of our Catholic values. And perhaps that's why Bryant is rushing our engagement. It's hard for a modern guy to wait almost a year before sex, even if he is Catholic.

"Arrrrgh!" I yell into the night.

Unable to feel my extremities, I curse my decision to run away to the cabin.

Why did I trust the Jeep would safely make this sixty-mile journey through the Alaskan wilderness? Last week the trip was easy.

There are no signs of life, no roadway markers, an endless expanse of snow-covered tundra far removed from the Alaskan highway system, and no cell towers out here. The cabin is even more remote, miles away from the dirt road.

If my rough calculations hold, I'm a mere two miles away. I *must* summon the strength to hike there.

I shut my eyes briefly, attempting to revive my frozen eyeballs, but darkness offers no respite. Despite my horrible situation, I'm not hypothermic—no confusion, hallucinations, or slurred speech.

I can make it. I WILL make it to the cabin!

At the cabin, I have my winter gear and a ready wood stove. But the looming question is, *what if I don't make it?*

My shaking body and my fast, shallow breaths urge me to hurry. *Dying is not an option!*

How can I be in this situation?

I should *be happy* in my *perfect* relationship with my new job, having a cozy holiday with my family—*not freezing to death alone in the dark tundra!*

Wilderness Rescue Series

Welcome to the breathtaking wilderness of Alaska, where love blooms as wild and beautiful as the northern lights.

Prepare for an exhilarating journey through diverse, LGBTQ+ inclusive romances set against the backdrop of charming small towns and untamed frontier.

Immerse yourself in a series that celebrates Alaskan culture and heartfelt relationships featuring trans, lesbian, bisexual, and two-spirit characters. From gripping rescues to soul-stirring connections, these standalone sapphic tales celebrate strong women navigating love and life with grit and determination in Alaska's rugged beauty.

Explore the standalone sapphic romance stories in the Wilderness Rescue Seriesat HarmonyNoble.com

"I loved learning more about Alaska... I also loved when they finally got their happy ending, it was super satisfying."**—Reviewer on Crashing Into Love**

She took the job in Alaska's wilderness to prove herself. Instead, her journey to love is the adventure.

City nurse Riley Thompson has her future perfectly mapped out—until she's stranded in a remote village. The only bright spot? The village elder who saved her life and sees right through her polished outer image.

Mary's wisdom as a Yu'pik elder has guided her people through countless storms, but talking a drunk pilot into landing safety—and saving a beautiful city nurse in the process—might be her greatest test yet.

With Riley's career pulling her back to city life?

Will tradition and personal ambition pull their hearts in opposite directions?

Join us at HarmonyNoble.com **to read this love story.**

"Unthaw My Heart" is a thrilling standalone novella to warm your heart and prove love reigns even in deadly conditions."

—Reviewer on Unthaw My Heart

In the harshest of winters, can a Christmas Eve storm turn two broken hearts into something beautiful?

Caught in a Christmas Eve blizzard, Dr. Makayla and Army mechanic Pauline are trapped in a remote Alaskan cabin—facing more than just the freezing cold. In the unforgiving wilderness of Alaska's Caribou Hills, survival is about opening your heart, facing your fears, and finding the strength to trust someone new.

As they navigate icy car crashes, broken promises, and the harsh realities of coming out in a town that feels too small, Paul and Mak discover that love is the one thing that can unthaw even the coldest hearts.

"This is my first Female/female romance I believed and I thought it was very cute and entertaining. The plot line was fresh and unique and I loved the characters."—**Reviewer on Winning Love**

Lights, camera, complication: Two coworkers team up to face off in Alaska's ultimate reality dating show, but when the game is love, who's really keeping score?

Stranded in Seldovia after their cruise jobs sink, Poppy and Baby join the outrageous new hit, The Smoking-Hot, Arctic Bachelor, scheming to win the cash and charm the hunky bachelor.

When prize and love collide, they flip the script, turning the romantic game show into a jaw-dropping celebration of true love.

Join us at HarmonyNoble.com **to read this love story.**

"A Riveting Rollercoaster of Love and Life in Alaska!" **—Reviewer on Stormy Hearts**

I steer my ship into the vast sea to lose my past. Instead, I found her. Now I chart a course to search for her lost love... A course that ends in my heartbreak.

In freezing Arctic waters, Maria's world shatters when her husband vanishes overboard, lost to the icy depths of Kachemak Bay. But fearless Alaskan boat captain, Jackie, swoops in to save her from the storm's clutches.

Despite Maria's grief and the town's judgment, their bond deepens, weaving a tale of love against the odds.

As they navigate through the stormy seas of prejudice and their own hidden pasts, they must choose—risk everything for love or let fear tear them apart?

Join us at HarmonyNoble.com **to read this love story and more when you** Embrace True Love!

"This novel is an absolute gem! The author skillfully weaves a romance that feels genuine and inclusive. Sterling and Chloe's love story is not just about love but also self-discovery and embracing life's unexpected twists..."**—Reviewer on Scoring Love**

Hockey was her game plan until love changed the rules.

In Fairbanks, where temperatures are at -66°F, a hockey star's perfectly planned life is about to get checked by love.

When hockey hotshot Sterling saves local artist, Chloe, from falling through the ice, neither expects the heat that ignites between them.

Can Sterling trade her player status for Chloe?

Will Chloe risk revealing that the coach tormenting Sterling is her ex-husband?

"I enjoyed the story a lot. . . some angst, and plenty of comic fun. I enjoy the insights into Alaskan life."—**Reviewer on Flooded Hearts**

In Alaska's wildest kitchen, a chef discovers that the best recipes can't be found in a cookbook when love is on the menu.

When uptight chef Lucy flees her toxic ex and lands in Cooper Landing, Alaska, she has one goal—becoming a Michelin-starred sensation.

Deb—beloved local farmer and keeper of indigenous traditions—believes any disaster can be fixed with wisdom and a community feast.

A flash flood threatens their tiny town, throwing these opposites together. Lucy—who doesn't do chaos or feelings—finds herself knee-deep in a rescue.
As her orderly life unravels, could messy, wholehearted Deb be exactly what she needs?

"A captivating journey of love and self-discovery that will stay with you long after you've turned the last page."

Sometimes the steepest mountains lead to the sweetest collisions-a story of skiing, healing, and love.

Get ready to race down the ski slopes where two paths cross on a wild ride of love and self-discovery.

Caitlyn, affectionately known as Cat, must overcome her inner turmoil and grumpiness to reclaim her belief in herself to find love.

Peekaboo is a dedicated ski instructor with an infectious zest for life that inspires others with disabilities to embrace joy and adventure. Yet, behind her smile is a heart yearning for more.

Torn between loyalty to her devoted partner and a longing for fiery passion, will Peekaboo choose love?

Join us at HarmonyNoble.com **to read this love story.**

"If you love opposites-attract romances that make your heart race, this is your next favorite book." **—Reviewer on Tides of Love**

Some days change your life forever. This is one of them.

Serena lives for adventure, but when a storm sweeps her into a dangerous rip tide off, she ends up stranded on a rocky outcropping, face-to-face with a cute, but unimpressed local.

Bree, a self-proclaimed Alaskan loner, wants nothing to do with the thrill-seeking surfer. But when the rising tide traps them, they'll have to rely on each other to survive.

What starts as a fight for survival turns into something much more—one storm, one day, and an undeniable connection that neither of them saw coming.

Join us at HarmonyNoble.com **to read this love story.**

"...If you are a fan of insta-love, this novella will be right up your alley. It is a cozy, sweet romance, with an exciting backdrop of the Alaskan Iditarod." **—Reviewer on Iditarod Love**

Love, survival, and the untamed Alaskan wilderness collide in the race of a lifetime.

Brace yourself for a thrilling journey on snow-swept trails of interior Alaska.

Brynn Dawson has ice in her veins and one goal—winning the Iditarod with her legendary dogsled team. But nothing prepares her for Morgan, an upbeat race volunteer with a knack for getting under her skin.

When disaster strikes during the start of the race on the crowded streets of Anchorage, their worlds collide in a daring rescue that ignites something neither of them saw coming.

COMING NEXT

Aurora's Wilderness Love
Hot Girl Summer Love

Where the odds are good, but the goods are odd—welcome to Alaska, to discover a love more untamed than the wilderness.

Aurora knows two things for certain: dating in Alaska is a contact sport, and survival isn't just about navigating frozen tundra—it's about navigating the heart. Broke, desperate, and one dating disaster away from giving up, she's determined to rewrite her story, one hilarious misstep at a time.

With more men than women in this last-frontier dating landscape, Aurora is about to discover that finding herself might be the greatest adventure of all. Armed with nothing but her wits, a killer sense of humor, and an uncanny ability to turn romantic catastrophes into comedy gold, she's ready to prove that sometimes love finds you when you least expect it—and usually when you look absolutely ridiculous.

Get ready for a heartwarming Alaskan rom-com where hunting for love is the ultimate wilderness sport, and Aurora is determined to bag her happily ever after.

The odds are good, the stories are better!

Snag the latest swoon-worthy read and find upcoming new releases at HarmonyNoble.com

Aurora's Wilderness Love
Just a Little Fall Crush

In Alaska, the ice is cold, but the workplace tension is scorching.

Aurora's back—and this time, she's juggling college, a corporate job she's barely qualified for, and a secret relationship with her infuriatingly poised boss. (Yes, that boss. The one with cheekbones sharp enough to slice through HR policy.)

After surviving the wilds of Alaskan dating, Aurora thought she knew chaos. But nothing prepared her for office romances, unread syllabi, and learning her absentee father might not be so absent after all. Between quarterly reports and unexpected DNA results, Aurora is forced to confront what it really means to grow up—and who gets to be called family.

With a found-family cast of coworkers, an all-too-supportive best friend, and a boss who kisses like a dream but critiques like a CEO, Aurora's once-simple survival plan turns into a rom-com of epic proportions. Can she keep her job and her heart intact—or will it all crash faster than her GPA?

Tropes you'll love: Secret workplace romance, "we shouldn't be doing this... but we are", found family in unexpected places, college girl chaos meets boss-level confidence, and a big emotional reveal with heartwarming fallout.

In a place where the moose outnumber the men, love was never going to be easy—but Aurora's about to learn that the greatest discoveries happen when you finally stop running and start showing up.

The odds are still good. The feelings? Even messier.

Aurora's Wilderness Love
Christmas Cruise Mistake

Escaping winter in Alaska? Check. Accidentally honeymooning with a stranger? Also check.

When a last-minute tropical Christmas cruise invite saves university student, Aurora, from an awkward post-break-up holiday and the freezing snow of Alaska, she packs her bikinis, her sass, and a plan to have fun and forget her epic break-up.

But a massive booking mix-up later, she's now pretending to be the runaway bride of the woman who left at the altar.

Oops!

Desperate and ready for a second-chance, Aurora's trapped on a couple's cruise filled with love exercises. Aurora's just trying to survive awkward icebreakers, too many trust falls, and the very real sparks flying with her accidental not-wife. *The plan? Fake it 'til they dock.*

A steamy karaoke duet changes everything. Aurora's heart is reignited and the cursed cruise might be what her tender heart needs.

Tangled in lies, tequila, and tension even a conga line can't break, Aurora's about to learn that running from romance leads her straight into the arms of a woman she never knew she needed.

The odds are still good. The drama? *It's a full-blown shipwreck.*

Other Titles by MELODY BEST
& HARMONY NOBLE

For the most up-to-date list visit
www.HarmonyNoble.com

Aurora's Wilderness Love:

Hot Girl Summer Love
Just a Little Fall Crush
Christmas Cruise Mistake

Wilderness Rescue Sapphic Romance Series:

Crashing Into Love
Unthaw My Heart
Winning Love
Stormy Hearts
Scoring Love
Flooded Hearts
Healing Hearts
Tides of Love
Iditarod Love
Frozen Hearts

Coffeehouse Romance Series:

Love, Joy & Lattes (Joy's Story)

Test Driving a Millionaire (Tara's Story)

Shattering Crystal a Bully Romance (Crystal's Story)

Choosing Love, Namaste (Meaghan's Story)

The Wrong Bride for Christmas (Monica's Story)

Coffeehouse Romance Short Stories:

Joy's 4th of July Holidate

Tara's Valentine Holidate

Crystal's Easter Holidate

Meaghan's New Year Holidate

Monica's Halloween Holidate

My Accidental Christmas Fiancé

Joy's Coffeehouse Romance

UNLOCK YOUR GIFT

Snag the latest swoon-worthy reads and stay tuned for upcoming stories at HarmonyNoble.com.

SERVINGS: 8 PREP TIME: 80 MIN COOK TIME: 10 MIN

Crunchy on the outside and soft on the inside, this yeast frybread is an Alaskan staple.

Ingredients

- 1 cup of milk, lukewarm
  (or 1/4 cup instant dry milk & warm water)
- 2 teaspoons yeast
  (or 1 envelope)
- 2 Tablespoons sugar
- 3-4 cups flour
- 1/2 teaspoon salt
- Shortening (or canola oil) for frying

Directions

1. Mix milk, yeast, & sugar in a large mixing bowl - set aside until the mixture forms a creamy foam layer on top, about 5 minutes.
2. Add salt to the yeast mixture, then slowly stir in 2 cups of flour. When adding the last of the flour, start kneading when you can no longer stir & add handfuls of flour until it forms a firm dough.
3. Move into a greased bowl, cover & let rise for one hour.
4. After it rises, punch it down, & split the dough into 8 pieces. Roll them into a ball, pat, & pull them flat.
5. Cut 3 - 4 lines through the dough & stretch it out slightly.
6. Heat 3 inches of oil in a deep-fryer or large saucepan to 350 degrees.
7. Gently place dough, one at a time, into the hot oil & fry until golden brown, turning once, 2 to 3 minutes per side.
8. Set on paper towels to drain.
9. Serve with a topping of your choice, such as powdered sugar, blueberry jam, honey, or cream cheese & salmon.
10. Enjoy!

About Author -
Harmony Noble & Melody Best

Meet the unstoppable twins from the rugged wilds of Alaska, the writing duo, Harmony & Melody. Fueled by endless lattes, their character-driven stories brim with authenticity, humor, and heart—featuring Alaskan grit, journeys of self-discovery, and swoon-worthy happily-ever-afters.

When they're not crafting adventure romances, these twins can be found hiking trails with breathtaking views, enjoying charming coffee shops, or exploring new worldwide destinations together.

Join the e-newsletter for exclusive content and give-aways at website: harmonynoble.com

Email: TrueLoveWriters@gmail.com
Instagram/Facebook/TikTok: @truelovewriters

www.ingramcontent.com/pod-product-compliance
Lightning Source LLC
LaVergne TN
LVHW010658110826
845149LV00014B/3148